FAMILY OF FALLEN LEAVES

EDITED BY CHARLES WAUGH AND HUY LIEN

FAMILY OF FALLEN LEAVES

STORIES OF AGENT ORANGE BY VIETNAMESE WRITERS

THE UNIVERSITY OF GEORGIA PRESS ATHENS AND LONDON

© 2010 by the University of Georgia Press

Athens, Georgia 30602

www.ugapress.org

All rights reserved

Designed by Mindy Basinger Hill

Set in 11.5/15.5 pt Garamond Premier Pro

Printed digitally in the United States of America

Library of Congress Cataloging-in-Publication Data

Family of fallen leaves : stories of Agent Orange by Vietnamese writers /
edited by Charles Waugh and Huy Lien.

     p.   cm.

A translated collection of Vietnamese fiction and nonfiction
about Agent Orange.

ISBN-13: 978-0-8203-3600-8 (hardcover : alk. paper)

ISBN-10: 0-8203-3600-9 (hardcover : alk. paper)

ISBN-13: 978-0-8203-3714-2 (pbk. : alk. paper)

ISBN-10: 0-8203-3714-5 (pbk. : alk. paper)

1. Agent Orange—Literary collections.

2. Herbicides—War use—Literary collections.

3. Vietnam War, 1961–1975—Chemical warfare—Literary collections.

4. Vietnamese literature—20th century—Translations into English.

I. Waugh, Charles, 1970– II. Lien, Huy.

PL4378.82.E5F35 2010

895.9'2209358597043—dc22   2010005977

British Library Cataloging-in-Publication Data available

This book is dedicated to everyone in Vietnam and the United States who suffers from exposure to chemical defoliants, and to the idea that together we can build a better future for our two countries.

Lá vàng còn ở trên cây,
Lá xanh rụng xuống trời hay không trời?

The yellow leaves are still on the tree,
But, God! have the green leaves already fallen?

VIETNAMESE FOLK SAYING

CONTENTS

FOREWORD

One evening in April 1973 when it was announced that the last American combat troops had left Vietnam, I remember sitting on the porch of the farmhouse that my wife and I rented near Penn State University, where I had been hired to teach after returning from the war. Sitting next to me was Bui Ngoc Huong, who, after four years and four surgeries to repair his destroyed mouth, was staying with us before undergoing his last reconstructive procedure in Philadelphia. It had been a warm day after a spring rain, and at dusk our empty little valley had begun to fill with fog. Then, from the hillside chapel across the creek and the gravel road, we heard the ringing of the church bell in its tiny belfry, the sound softened by the evening mist.

"What's that about?" Huong asked.

I explained that a parishioner had gone to ring the bell because our soldiers were coming home. It was a custom. Peace, I said, might be coming to Vietnam. Like most people, with the signing of the Paris Peace Accords, I thought our long war would soon be over.

Huong was sixteen, had grown a foot on American food, and wore his hair long in the cool style of the day. His father was a South Vietnamese soldier who had been killed in battle. His mother had run off with another soldier, putting Huong in a seaside orphanage near Da Nang. At the orphanage, playing with other kids on the beach, he had picked up a strange object and for some reason touched it to his tongue. It exploded. He had found a Dragon's Tooth, a "scatterable" landmine, smaller than a child's hand, sown by air, which took off the front his of mouth and lower jaw. In the U.S., he had been placed with American foster families as he recovered from surgeries that had left him with a working mouth and brownish lips fashioned from a skin graft. When I first saw Huong at the orphanage, he was holding a hand mirror to locate the small hard hole that was then his mouth and trying to feed himself by stuffing soft food into the opening. Now, four years later, my wife and I were his last foster family before his final surgery and his going home to his grandmother, his only living relative.

Huong thought a minute, then asked, "Is it peace or only a bell ringing?"

Wars, as we continue to forget, do not end when the last shot is fired. The hostile nations, winners and losers, are changed forever as soldiers come back altered, damaged, or not at all. Their families are changed. Slowly or quickly, these domestic changes reverberate through societies as the economic and personal costs continue to be paid long after the shooting stops. In ancient China, generals returning home with their armies reentered the capital through a gate of mourning. This was true whether the campaign had been a success or a defeat because war is a pollution and ceremonies are required to protect the living from the inevitable spiritual consequences.

During the Vietnam War, I volunteered as a civilian conscientious objector and worked as the field representative for the Committee of Responsibility, a volunteer group of doctors and lay people who sought to bring the most severely wounded children to medical care. The children that we brought to hospitals in Saigon or airlifted to major teaching hospitals in the U.S. were riddled by bullets, slashed by cluster bomb flechettes, blinded and deafened by tossed grenades, had spines severed, and had lost their limbs. One boy had his chin glued to his chest by napalm. One girl had her face burnt and her eyelids scorched off by a white phosphorus artillery shell. One gunshot toddler survived the massacre of her family in a ditch because she was protected by their bodies.

During the war I often traveled from Saigon to regional hospitals to speak to referring doctors, or to bring passport paperwork to the children's families, or to accompany these children on airplanes and ambulances to hospital beds in Saigon before their long trip to the United States. Sometimes Vietnamese or American military doctors would ask me to bring back with me to Saigon other children scheduled for corrective surgery. Once I accompanied five children with cleft lips and palates. They weren't considered war-injured, just unfortunately deformed. Now we know better. Cleft palatism, along with spina bifida, other gross malformations, and Down Syndrome, can be caused by Agent Orange or, more accurately, by the teratogenic dioxin by-product in the herbicide.

From 1961 to 1971, the United States sprayed some 20 million gallons of herbicides on the mountain and mangrove forests, paddy tree lines, and waterways of Vietnam, exposing millions of people—including thousands of American soldiers—to dioxin. Dow Chemical and Monsanto, as well as military authorities, knew from the outset that the dioxin in their herbicides could cause cancer and birth malformations and, later, a devastating host of skin and neurological symptoms.

Now we know that the wartime spraying was only the first stage of the contamination. When our troops came home, our herbicide depots were simply abandoned, leaving dioxin to leak into the ground and enter into the plant and animal life of the countryside for decades. For those Vietnamese and their children afflicted by exposure to dioxin, the war has not ended and no assuaging bell has tolled, as dioxin contamination continues to destroy lives in Vietnam.

Here is a brief description of dioxin's effects, as posted on the World Health Organization Web site:

> Dioxins are environmental pollutants. They have the dubious distinction of belonging to the "dirty dozen"—a group of dangerous chemicals known as persistent organic pollutants. Dioxins are of concern because of their highly toxic potential. Experiments have shown they affect a number of organs and systems. Once dioxins have entered the body, they endure a long time because of their chemical stability and their ability to be absorbed by fat tissue, where they are then stored in the body. Their half-life in the body is estimated to be seven to eleven years. In the environment, dioxins tend to accumulate in the food chain. The higher in the animal food chain one goes, the higher is the concentration of dioxins.

This collection of short stories and nonfiction lets us hear the voices of people directly affected by the continuing destruction of what Vietnamese call the American War. One can only praise its editors for going to great efforts to gather these stories: two literature professors, Charles Waugh, from Utah State University, and Huy Lien, professor emeritus from the National University in Hanoi.

The Vietnamese authors of these stories are mostly ex-soldiers, women and men from farming communities, who went off to war as youngsters. Later, they became editors and writers. Once they might have become collateral damage, or enemy KIA. In postwar Vietnam they became writers.

It's time, past time, to hear their stories.

John Balaban, PROFESSOR AND POET-IN-RESIDENCE
NORTH CAROLINA STATE UNIVERSITY, RALEIGH

PREFACE

We have titled this collection *Family of Fallen Leaves* to evoke the main themes found in all the narratives: family, the interconnectedness of all living things, and of course, defoliation. Despite these common threads, the narratives remain surprisingly varied, each adding some element all the more poignant for its unpredictability.

For example, Suong Nguyet Minh weaves the tale of "Thirteen Harbors" around two unexpected bits of Vietnamese culture, the proverb *A girl has twelve harbors* and a legend about a snake princess. Ranging from the history of the Vietnamese struggle against the Cham in the tenth century A.D. to the history of the American War, this story helps us see the centuries-long Vietnamese struggle for autonomy and independence, as well as the hardships faced by the countless women whose husbands went to war. But we cannot forget that Minh has twined this exciting weft of history and folklore through the more understated warp of family integrity. In fact, the conviction that couples should marry and have children to preserve the family name, care for their parents in old age, and continue the tradition of honoring their ancestors is so important—such an unquestioned, fundamental part of Vietnamese life, culture, and language—that "Thirteen Harbors," and all the stories in the collection, take it as a given. Sometimes this essential family integrity remains intact, sometimes, tragically, it does not.

Both "The Goat Horn Bell," by Nguyen Quang Lap, and "A Dream," by Phan Ngoc Tien, explore all the typical hopes and fears a husband and wife feel when trying to become pregnant or expecting a child, but the stories also demonstrate how those typical fears are compounded immensely by the added terrifying factor of having been exposed to dioxin. How those fears, when coupled with the strong desire—or sometimes the social obligation—to have children, lead parents to make bad decisions is examined in Nguyen Thi Ngoc Ha's "The Spirit Pond," as well as in Hoang Minh Tuong's "Grace." Under very different circumstances, both stories explore how women become trapped by their parents' desires to maintain propriety and preserve their family line.

Of course, a parent's worry doesn't end at childbirth. Hoang Minh Tuong's "The Story of a Family" and Minh Chuyen's "A Father and His Children" track families through several generations and demonstrate how difficult it is for families to endure physical separation, war, the struggle to put food on the table, and the additional suffering from dioxin exposure. Having made many visits to such families with dioxin researcher Dr. Le Cao Dai, Minh Chuyen often features this intergenerational aspect of dioxin exposure in his essays and stories.

Trung Trung Dinh's story "Love Forest" recognizes that to be parents a couple first must find one another, fall in love, and manage to stay together. It underscores that dioxin exposure disrupted lives in more ways than one would imagine and that people continue to suffer even though the war is long over. Vo Thi Hao's "The Blood of Leaves" comes to a similar conclusion, helping us to understand how a single life touches many others. When one person dies because of dioxin exposure, the effect ripples throughout the community.

Such unexpected connections are the theme of several stories, most notably Thu Tran's "The Quiet Poplar" and Ma Van Khang's "Thay Phung" and "A Child, a Man." Thu Tran is a native of Bien Hoa, the site of one of Operation Ranch Hand's largest bases and, therefore, one of the places in Vietnam still most polluted with dioxin. She thus can easily be imagined as the protagonist of "The Quiet Poplar"—someone who is not known to be directly affected by dioxin but who has lived right next door to those who have, and wants to do something to help. Having grown up knowing of the many lives lost to dioxin on Bien Hoa's Sixth Street—the one nearest the airport and, therefore, the most contaminated with dioxin—she wrote the story with "characters inspired by the tragic situation of the many people who live on that street. I imagined myself as a victim like them." Similarly, Ma Van Khang uses a protagonist in "A Child, a Man" who is not affected by dioxin to wonder how life can go on for a neighboring family that is. As he and Thu Tran have intuited, the only way to provide help for the suffering is to begin with an act of the imagination, a leap into the experience of another.

This highly charged moment of empathy sits at the core of all the writers' responses to the challenge of Agent Orange exposure. Their work allows readers to think, live, and suffer vicariously as a person exposed and to identify with that person and establish a deeply felt human connection. Various documentary films and photograph collections have done much to publicize the visual horror of Agent Orange exposure, but where they motivate through alienation—healthy human beings simply should not look like that—these stories motivate through affiliation. They bring the reader inside the mind of someone coping with exposure, bridging the gap between those who suffer and those who can help.

More broadly, as works of the imagination, these stories and essays reflect the way that Agent Orange has continued to linger in the Vietnamese unconscious. Just as dioxin has persisted in the environment, continuing to poison people even to this day, it has also continued to weigh heavily on Vietnamese minds, haunting their hopes for the future, reminding them of the injustice of the war, and preventing a final and full reconciliation with the United States. Only when this issue has been thoroughly addressed and redressed can our two nations finally move forward together.

To that end, we have arranged these works from those that cannot yet see hope for solving this challenge to those that do. From those that chronicle the deepest lows to those that imagine powerful interventions by caring Vietnamese and Americans that substantially improve the lives of the exposed. We hope our readers will walk away from this collection with the writers' same power to imagine themselves as a person exposed to dioxin and with the same impetus to join their talents with the many others who have answered the call for assistance.

In collaborating on these translations, we had similar aspirations. Our team consisted of three native Vietnamese speakers and one native English speaker. We began with a rough translation into English, followed by a rigorous process of working back toward a literal word-for-word translation that matched the original Vietnamese syntax and sentence structure. Finally, the last stage involved honing the English prose until it was as concise and sharp as the original Vietnamese while at the same time achieving an immediate clarity of meaning. Since so much of Vietnamese is contextual and implied, often omitting parts of a sentence that are integral to English, this was not always easy. The Vietnamese proverb mentioned above, *"A girl has twelve harbors,"* is a good example. The original Vietnamese, "Con gái mười hai bến nước," literally means "girl twelve riverports," which by itself would mean very little to an English speaking audience—it doesn't even have a verb! But through our collaboration, we hope we have surmounted the challenge sufficiently to allow native English speakers to see the world in a Vietnamese way and to be as moved as we were by each of these narratives.

ACKNOWLEDGMENTS

The editors would like to thank all the writers whose work has been translated here, as well as the many others whose assistance was integral to producing this book. We would also like to thank the Rockefeller Foundation and the William Joiner Center, whose support for this project helped get it off the ground. Finally, our deepest gratitude goes to our families, whose patience and encouragement has sustained us throughout.

FAMILY OF FALLEN LEAVES

CHARLES WAUGH

INTRODUCTION

Between August 10, 1961, and January 7, 1971, the United States military sprayed approximately 20 million gallons of chemical defoliants on roughly 6,000 square miles of Vietnam's jungles, croplands, and waterways, exposing millions of people to the defoliants' toxic byproduct, dioxin. Many of those sprayed directly were poor, rural people, ethnic minorities living in Vietnam's highlands or the Vietnamese soldiers and youth brigades operating in the Southern jungles and along supply routes from the North. But others sprayed included U.S. soldiers themselves and their allies from South Korea, Australia, New Zealand, and the Philippines. Still more were exposed in the actual process of spraying: Vietnamese and Americans assigned to load and unload the toxic chemicals from ship or plane to onshore storage areas and into the spraying apparatuses. After the war, when the exposed returned to their homes all around the world and began to have children, many of them unwittingly passed on the genetic damage the dioxin had wrought, increasing the disaster's effects to global, multigenerational proportions.

The Department of Veterans Affairs recognizes and compensates 7,500 American veterans for fifteen diseases associated with Agent Orange exposure, including immediate effects such as chloracne and peripheral neuropathy; delayed effects such as type II diabetes, prostate cancer, and Hodgkin's disease; and intergenerational effects such as spina bifida and other birth defects. However, the U.S. has not officially recognized any obligation to the Vietnamese who suffer similar illnesses. Though we have yet to see what attitude the

Obama administration will adopt, past administrations have dismissed out of hand the claims of Vietnamese suffering from Agent Orange-related illnesses, asserting they are based on, as former U.S. Ambassador to Vietnam Ray Burghardt put it, "fake science."[1] To make matters worse, because of sovereign immunity, the U.S. Government can refuse to allow itself to be sued for crimes committed by its military, leaving unpunished the decision to spray the defoliants and to endanger the lives of its enemies and allies alike.

In the meantime, engaged advocacy groups, artists, writers, and ordinary citizens from around the world have attempted to raise awareness about Agent Orange exposure, rally support for the exposed, and begin to solve this complicated problem.

A BRIEF ENVIRONMENTAL HISTORY
OF OPERATION RANCH HAND

From the very beginning in Professor E. J. Kraus's laboratory at the University of Chicago when each day for several weeks he ingested one gram of the defoliant 2,4-D to "prove" it held no danger to humans, to the actual application of Agent Orange at up to twenty-five times the concentrations allowed for similar commercial products in the U.S., government scientists and the military ignored the precautionary principle, demonstrating a casualness toward dangerous chemicals possible only in the kind of thoroughly petro- and organo-chemical-saturated culture found in the U.S. since World War II. In fact, the purpose of the defoliant program's most rigorous testing before large-scale deployment merely confirmed the necessary concentrations to strip jungle foliage with one pass of the specially modified C-123 cargo planes. Despite foreknowledge of the presence of dioxin contamination in the defoliants, not a single test measured how much dioxin would be delivered, how it would pass through or affect watersheds, how it would enter the food chain, or what would happen to humans exposed to high levels of dioxin.[2]

To make matters worse, by 1965, when Ranch Hand was in full swing, the military's enormous demand for defoliants prompted the thirty-seven manufacturers of Agent Orange to forgo production safety measures that could have kept the dioxin contamination at the levels approved for domestic sales. Tetrachlorodibenzo-p dioxin (TCDD) is the most toxic of all the different types of dioxin and a byproduct in both of the chemical ingredients of Agent Orange: 2,4-dichlorophenoxyacetic acid (2,4-D) and 2,4,5-trichlorophenoxy-acetic acid (2,4,5-T). The hotter and faster the defoliant is produced, the more it is contaminated by dioxin. Production standards at times became so lax that dioxin levels soared to fifty times the domestic industry standard.[3]

Dioxin is known to cause birth defects in mice, and in humans cancer, type II diabetes, chloracne, reproductive and developmental effects, impaired immune systems, behavioral changes, and endo-crine effects.[4] According to Dr. James Clary, one of the defoliation program scientists, there is no doubt the military knew the risks they were taking for human health: "When we initiated the herbicide program in the 1960s, we were aware of the potential for damage due to dioxin contamination in the herbicide. We were even aware that the 'military' formulation had a higher dioxin concentration than the 'civilian' version due to the lower cost and speed of manufacture. However, because the material was to be used on the 'enemy,' none of us were overly concerned."[5] And yet common sense would suggest that using something so dangerous might actually constitute chemi-cal warfare or, at the very least, that using something so dangerous for the enemy might also endanger the men assigned to spray it.

But the military's method for addressing this concern simply sug-gests a kind of racism and classism inherent at the institutional level.

Only enlisted men, who during the draft years of the war in Vietnam were disproportionately from poor and minority communities, were assigned the tasks involved with the loading and unloading of the defoliants and maintenance of the spray units. Worse, Admiral Harry Felt, Commander in Chief, Pacific (CINCPAC), clearly understood the defoliants posed some danger when he ordered that "Vietnamese personnel will be utilized to the maximum extent possible in the handling of chemicals for the defoliant operation to include delivery of defoliants to the spray aircraft."[6] This order forced the Vietnamese to bear the highest risk for exposure since the handling involved direct and sustained contact with the dioxin at its highest, undiluted levels.

By Ranch Hand's end, the operation had delivered the World Health Organization's maximum "safe" daily intake of dioxin for the average Vietnamese 39,855 times for every square foot sprayed,[7] and that figure does not take into account the dioxin from the defoliants that leaked or were otherwise dumped at the several storage sites scattered across the southern half of the country.

GLOBAL DISPERSAL

Even after the war, the dioxin initially stored and sprayed in Vietnam continued to circulate, having persisted in the environment and bioaccumulated its way up the food chain. Defoliated croplands returned to production with dioxin-contaminated soil. Cows and buffalo ate contaminated plant material and stored the dioxin in their fat. Frogs and fish absorbed significant amounts of dioxin from the sediment in the water they lived in. Scavengers unwittingly transported discarded defoliant barrels far from their storage sites and converted them into water tanks. And the vast amounts of dioxin that had entered the soils of the Ranch Hand airbases began a slow but steady flow into the surrounding watersheds. In 2006, soil samples from bases at Bien Hoa and Da Nang tested positive for dioxin at 1 million ppt and 365,000 ppt respectively, 1,000 times and 365 times the Agency for Toxic Substances and Disease Registry's maximum acceptable limit of 1,000 ppt.[8]

And of course, dioxin also moved inside human bodies. Vietnamese civilian refugees, volunteers, and soldiers alike returned home after the war, often traveling all the way across the country. Many of them knew immediately upon exposure to Agent Orange that something was wrong. Symptoms such as chloracne, porphyria cutanea tarda, and peripheral neuropathy manifest within a week or up to a year after exposure. But many others did not find out or suspect anything until later, when they got older and became ill or, worse, when their children were born deformed or were lost before birth.

Many South Vietnamese soldiers left Vietnam after 1975, taking their exposure-related illnesses with them all over the world. Similarly, thousands of soldiers from the U.S., Australia, New Zealand, South Korea, and the Philippines returned home after the war, carrying dioxin inside their bodies. Like their former enemies, they soon began to discover that making it home alive did not mean they had survived the war.

Complicating the dispersal of Agent Orange's dioxin still further, in 1977 the Dutch ship *Vulcanus* picked up the remaining U.S. stockpile at Gulfport, Mississippi, transported it to the North Pacific via the Panama Canal, and incinerated it along with the defoliants that had been removed from Vietnam to a holding area on Johnston Atoll. The Air Force had briefly considered straining the dioxin from the defoliants using activated charcoal but was stymied by what to do with the toxic charcoal byproduct.[9] By choosing incineration, they allowed themselves to believe the dioxin simply disappeared. As we now know, dioxin incinerated in the northern hemisphere often reformulates in the upper atmosphere and then migrates toward the pole, bioaccumulating up fatty food chains into predators such as polar bears and seals and into arctic peoples such as the Nunavit.[10]

LEGAL ACTION

Because the U.S. Government can refuse to allow itself to be sued for damages incurred while fighting a war, the exposed have not been able to hold it directly responsible, even though the government ultimately made the decision to spray, as well as all the subsidiary decisions about how the spraying would happen and to what extent the chemical companies with whom it had contracted would be held to normal production safeguards. Instead, the exposed have been forced to focus their efforts on the chemical companies that allowed the dioxin content in the defoliants to rise so dramatically.

In 1978 American veterans filed a class action lawsuit against seven of the Agent Orange manufacturers. Six years later, the chemical companies settled the suit for $180 million just before it went to trial, without admitting liability. One of the companies, Dow, issued a statement explaining that the settlement reflected a "'compassionate, expedient and productive means' of meeting the needs of all parties," and argued that it had decided to settle since, "despite the strength of the scientific case, it would be difficult for the jury to sort out the issues in this highly emotional case."[11] In other words, they knew they would have a hard time finding a jury not sympathetic to the idea that the Americans who had fought in Vietnam had been victimized enough already, whether the science could prove the manufacturers' culpability or not. The settlement distributed up to $12,000 for each American, New Zealander, and Australian veteran who tested positive for dioxin exposure and had been classified as 100 percent disabled by the VA. A second lawsuit, filed by the veterans' families against the U.S. military, was dismissed on the grounds that the plaintiffs offered no evidence linking Agent Orange to the illnesses cited.

By 1999, the science had caught up with what the victims knew intuitively, and the twenty thousand South Korean veterans who had been left out of the 1984 settlement in the U.S. filed a suit against the Agent Orange producers in a South Korean court, seeking more than $5 billion in damages. Though the veterans lost the case in 2002, they appealed, and in January 2006 the appellate court awarded damages ranging from $6,200 to $47,500 to about 6,800 veterans and their survivors, totaling nearly $63 million. The chemical companies appealed, and as of yet no payments have been made.[12]

In 2003, Vietnamese doctors, veterans, and others exposed formed the Vietnamese Association of Victims of Agent Orange—VAVA—in Hanoi to concentrate efforts to provide medical assistance and rehabilitation. The following January, VAVA filed a lawsuit in United States District Court against the chemical companies using the Alien Tort Claims Act, alleging that the manufacturers' knowledge of the high levels of dioxin in the herbicides along with the knowledge that it would be sprayed in such a way as to contaminate human beings and their food supplies constituted "violations of international law and war crimes."[13]

In March 2005, Judge Jack Weinstein (the Brooklyn district court judge who had overseen the American veterans' 1984 settlement and the failed 1985 suit against the U.S. military) dismissed the case, arguing no law between 1961 and 1971 prohibited the wartime use of defoliants, ignoring altogether that VAVA's claim was against the recklessly high levels of dioxin in the defoliants, not the defoliants themselves. VAVA's appeal was heard in June 2007, but the appeals court again ignored the claim against the presence of high levels of dioxin, approached the question simply from the standpoint that the

U.S. had not agreed not to use defoliants at that time, and upheld the decision. In 2008, VAVA appealed to the Supreme Court, which declined to hear the case in March 2009.

ADVOCACY

Though the legal process has not been particularly successful, the exposed have received some relief through advocacy and political action. In 1975, largely as a result of the growing public condemnation of the defoliation program, Gerald Ford issued executive order 11850, prohibiting the military use of chemical defoliants, and the Senate finally found the impetus to ratify the 1925 Geneva protocol banning chemical weapons. In 1991, thanks to the advocacy of the Vietnam Veterans of America Foundation (which is now called Veterans for America [VFA]), George H. W. Bush signed the Agent Orange Act of 1991, authorizing a long-term health study on defoliant exposure. Since then, the study's findings have been released at a minimum of every two years and have helped to get several associated diseases added to the list of those eligible for compensation and care from the VA. In addition to the Veterans' Health Care Eligibility Reform Act of 1996 guaranteeing VA care to veterans exposed to defoliants, at present the VA recognizes and compensates for fifteen major illnesses associated with service-related dioxin poisoning. In all, nearly 300,000 American veterans have had Agent-Orange-related health exams, and over 99,000 have filed claims alleging exposure-related illnesses, but only 7,520 actually receive disability compensation.[14] Veterans made many of these gains in spite of resistance from the VA, which for many years refused to take the veterans' health claims seriously for the incredible reason that no studies had yet been done to corroborate them.

The American veterans' effort to make the government take

responsibility for the aftermath of Agent Orange has even begun, finally, to apply to Vietnam. Thanks to the advocacy of the VFA, the Ford Foundation, and others, in May 2007 the U.S. Congress appropriated $3 million for cleaning up dioxin hotspots at the old airbases in Vietnam. Though the amount is not enough even to clean up one hotspot (the estimate for the remediation of the site at Da Nang alone is $17 million) and the language of the bill takes no responsibility for having caused the problem, it is a start.[15]

Some of the best news resulting from advocacy came in the summer of 2007, when the Ford Foundation announced the formation of the U.S.-Vietnam Dialogue Group on Agent Orange/Dioxin, pledging $7.5 million to fund: 1) the remediation of dioxin hotspots around former U.S. airbases; 2) the support of treatment and education centers; 3) the establishment of a Vietnamese laboratory for dioxin testing, including staff training; 4) the creation of training courses for local communities on land restoration; and 5) general issue education and advocacy.[16] Aside from contributing funds, the involvement of such widely respected and highly influential organizations as the Ford Foundation and the Aspen Institute suggests that considerable pressure might be brought to bear on the U.S. Government to find an appropriate solution to the problem.

In Vietnam in the mid-1990s, largely because of the attention writers and journalists drew to the plight of veterans sick and dying from exposure, the National Assembly enacted a special pension to support dioxin victims with between five and twenty-five dollars each month, which, though meager, at the very least could provide enough to feed a rural family. Since then, political support for the victims has continued to grow. Nursing homes and orphanages specifically for dioxin victims have been opened, children of victims receive free educations, victims who can still work are given priority for small business loans, and all are given priority access to medical care. The Vietnam Red Cross, which is overseen by the National Assembly, coordinates international and domestic aid and has channeled over $5.3 million in the last eight years toward dioxin relief, providing wheelchairs, housing, food subsidies, medical care, orthopedic surgery, and physical rehabilitation. Also in 2004, one of the primary political organizations in Vietnam, the Fatherland Front Central Committee, established a day of remembrance, August 10 — the date of the first spray mission in 1961 — as a Day for Agent Orange victims.[17]

CULTURAL INFLUENCE

In many ways, these successes, including the 1984 settlement, were made possible by the way in which cultural responses to Agent Orange exposure shaped public opinion. For example, in the U.S., the issue of Agent Orange was one of many that, as Marita Sturken has argued, established "Vietnam veterans as the primary victims of the war."[18] During this period, the beleaguered image of the American Vietnam veteran came to the forefront of American cultural life. In 1982, the same year the Vietnam Veterans Memorial was completed, the movie *First Blood* did just as much, if not more, to establish the primacy of the American veteran's victimhood since far more people saw the film than made a visit to the memorial in Washington, D.C. And though Agent Orange does not figure very much into *First Blood*'s plot, the movie's opening scene does revise David Morrell's original 1972 novel to show John Rambo trying to find his sole remaining combat buddy, Delmar Barry, only to learn from Barry's wife, who is folding laundry with her children playing in the yard behind her, that he, too, is dead, the largest man in the unit "brought down to nothing" by cancer resulting from exposure to Agent Orange. The news crushes Rambo as he realizes that with this death his country has finally taken everything from him. It is this added scene, with Agent Orange exposure presented as a kind of last straw, a final "gotcha," that sets up everything else. The coinciding sense of victimhood the film develops throughout cannot be dismissed when reading the Dow spokesman's rationalization for the 1984 settlement that "it would be difficult for the jury to sort out the issues in this highly emotional case."[19]

Along with the two novels that loosely associate American Vietnam-era veterans' victimization with exposure to Agent Orange—Bobbie Ann Mason's *In Country* and Stephen Wright's *Meditations in Green*—*First Blood* and the dozen or so non-Agent Orange related Vietnam war films of the 1980s all contributed to a consensus in American culture and politics that whatever could be done for the American veterans of the war in Vietnam should be. It was this popular consensus that made U.S. Agent Orange advocacy successful and the 1984 settlement possible, even when the science had not yet been able to explain the illnesses and their pathways.

Vietnamese writers, however, could not allow themselves to approach the issue of Agent Orange from the metaphorical distance employed by writers such as Wright and Mason. For them, the suffering caused by Agent Orange was tangible, real, and pervasive: more than 2 million Vietnamese currently receive an Agent Orange benefit from the government, and it is estimated that more than 3 million suffer from related illnesses with various degrees of debilitation. Many of those 3 million are the children and grandchildren of the men and women initially exposed. In a country of approximately 89 million, that's more than 3 percent of the present-day population.[20]

As early as 1984, well before Vietnam's National Assembly established Agent Orange pensions, writer Ma Van Khang had begun to wonder about the fate of the exposed. In his short story "A Child, a Man," he tells about a boy whose stepmother suffers from cancer and psychosis due to her wartime service when she was sprayed repeatedly while repairing roads along the Ho Chi Minh trail. Her illness compels her to abuse the child, who seeks refuge in the narrator's home. Though the story tends mainly to build sympathy for the child, the stepmother's vulnerability works as a kind of epiphany at the end, where Khang leaves the reader wondering along with the narrator, "How could that woman ever recover from such an illness?"

Vietnamese writers took up this question repeatedly over the next two decades, including journalist Minh Chuyen, whose widely published essays helped bring the fate of the exposed into mainstream political and social discourse. By repeatedly placing the everyday lives of people suffering from dioxin exposure—their poverty, their hopelessness, their service to the country—in the pages of the national newspapers, his essays ultimately helped garner the political pressure to provide relief.

Family of Fallen Leaves collects the writers of Vietnam's answers to Khang's question for the first time in one place. It is Huy Lien's and my hope, along with the hope of all the writers who cooperated with us in this project, that these stories will have the same kind of transformative power in the United States as they had in Vietnam and that the American works had for the cause of American veterans. It is difficult, after reading them and having the vicarious experience of thinking, living, and suffering as someone exposed, not to identify with and admire these Vietnamese victims of Agent Orange. Above all else, these are stories of survival, of a people with an indomitable spirit that cannot be crushed, no matter how difficult the circumstances.

Given the conservative nature of the 2009 U.S. Supreme Court, few people outside of Vietnam really believed VAVA's appeal of the 2007 Federal Court decision would succeed. But the case did raise the profile of the problem somewhat, and while justice can be sought as an ideal, what really matters is making a substantial difference in the many lives of those who still do not have enough to eat, who receive inadequate medical care, and who spend their days in terrible pain with little hope for a better tomorrow. Americans cannot take the dioxin from the bodies of the exposed, but we can clean up the land; we can offer financial and medical assistance; and we can pass legislation to ensure it never happens again. As the successful advocacy for the $3 million appropriation to help remediate the Da Nang airbase has demonstrated, when enough people understand and empathize with the suffering of others, anything is possible.

If after reading these stories you would like to do something to help, contact your local representative in Congress, contact the V FA and make a donation for Agent Orange advocacy, or contribute to one of the Agent Orange advocacy groups listed below.

Vietnamese Victims of Agent Orange: http://www.vava.org.vn

Veterans for America: http://www.veteransforamerica.org

Fund for Reconciliation and Development: http://www.ffrd.org

Friendship Village: http://www.vietnamfriendship.org

War Legacies Project: http://www.warlegacies.org

NOTES

1. Ray Burghardt in a discussion with Fulbright grantees, U.S. Embassy, Hanoi, 27 August 2004.

2. V. K. Rowe, Dow Biochemical Research Laboratory, to Ross Milholland, manager Dow Bioproducts, memorandum, 24 June 1965. This memorandum from one of Dow's scientists to its management discusses the high level of dioxin in the defoliants it had produced, recognizes the threat exposure would pose to human health, and suggests cleaning "up our own house from within, rather than having someone from without do it for us" before restrictive legislation is passed. The letter was marked "confidential" with a postscript at the bottom reading: "P.S. Under no circumstances may this letter be reproduced, shown, or sent to anyone outside of Dow." It was made public during the lawsuit the Vietnamese Victims of Agent Orange brought against the chemical companies in 2003.

3. Combined with the higher application concentrations, that means frequently $50 \times 25 = 1,250$ times the acceptable amount of dioxin was being delivered. Arnold Schector et al., "Dioxins: An Overview," *Environmental Research* 101 (2006): 419. *VAVA v. Dow*, 04 CV 0400, U.S. District Court, Brooklyn, N.Y., 2003.

4. Environmental Protection Agency, "2001 Toxics Release Inventory Data Release Questions and Answers," http://www.epa.gov/tri/tridata/tri01/external _qanda_for_revision.pdf.

5. Dr. James R. Clary to Senator Tom Daschle, 9 September 1988. Reproduced in E. R. Zumwalt, *Report to Secretary of the Department of Veterans Affairs on the Association between Adverse Health Effects and Exposure to Agent Orange* (Washington: Department of Veterans Affairs, 1990), 6.

6. Admiral Harry Felt, "Telegram from the Commander in Chief, Pacific (Felt), to the Chief of the Military Assistance Advisory Group in Vietnam (McGarr)"/1/ Honolulu, 28 December 1961, 12:45 p.m., Washington National Records Center, RG 84, Saigon Embassy Files: FRC 68 A 5159, GVN January-June 1962. Top Secret. Repeated to the Joint Chiefs of Staff, JACK AJCC, PACAF, and Navy GRNC. http://www.state.gov/www/about_state/history/ vol_i_1961/zc.html.

7. The World Health Organization recommends no greater exposure than 1 picogram per each kilogram of body weight per day; with the average Vietnamese weighing 45 kg, that's 45 picograms per day. Distributing the estimated 400-plus kilograms of dioxin that was delivered over the area sprayed means that each square foot sprayed received 39,855 times the WHO's maximum recommended daily exposure. Put another way, each square foot sprayed received enough dioxin to poison one Vietnamese person with the WHO's maximum "safe" amount each day for 109 years.

8. Arnold Schector et al., "Agent Orange and the Vietnamese: The Persistence of Elevated Dioxin Levels in Human Tissues," *American Journal of Public Health* 85 (April 1995): 516–17. Hatfield Consultants, *Assessment of Dioxin Contamination in the Environment and Human Population in the Vicinity of Da Nang Airbase, Vietnam, Report 3: Final Report* (West Vancouver, B.C.: Hatfield Consultants, 2007), 2–3.

9. William A. Buckingham Jr., *Operation Ranch Hand: The Air Force and Herbicides in Southeast Asia, 1961–1971* (Washington: Office of Air Force History, USAF, 1982), 189.

10. Barry Commoner et al., "Long-range Air Transport of Dioxin from North American Sources to Ecologically Vulnerable Receptors in Nunavut, Arctic Canada," *Final Report to the North American Commission for Environmental Cooperation*, http://www.cec.org/pubs_docs/documents/index .cfm?varlan=english&ID=73, 73.

11. Ralph Blumenthal, "Veterans Accept $180 Million Pact on Agent Orange," *New York Times*, 8 May 1984.

12. Jae-Soon Chang, "South Korean Court Orders Two U.S. Companies to Pay Damages over Agent Orange," *Associated Press Worldstream*, 26 January 2006. Len Aldis, director of the Vietnam–Britain Friendship Society, e-mail message to the author, 25 January 2007.

13. Vietnamese Victims of Agent Orange, home page, http://www.vava .org.vn/.

14. Environmental Agents Service, Department of Veterans Affairs, "Agent Orange General Information Brochure," July 2003, Department of Veterans Affairs, http://www1.va.gov/agentorange/docs/AOIB10 – 49JUL03.pdf. Department of Veterans Affairs, "Vietnam Veteran Factsheet," Department

of Veterans Affairs, http://www.vba.va.gov/bln/21/Milsvc/Docs/VNFacts .doc.

15. Wayne Dwernychuk, e-mail message to the author, 20 January 2009. Dr. Dwernychuk is a retired but still active consultant in the Hatfield Group, which is cooperating with the Vietnamese military to remediate the site in Da Nang. Veterans for America, "VFA's Drive Program," Veterans for America, http://www.veteransforamerica.org/programs/postconflict/vietnam/vvaf-in-vietnam.html.

16. Ford Foundation, "Joint Humanitarian Group Is Launched to Build Support to Overcome Agent Orange Legacies," http://www.fordfound.org/ newsroom/pressreleases/201.

17. "Assistance for Vietnamese Agent Orange Victims," *Thai Press Reports*, 18 May 2005. Big donors included the International Federation of Red Cross and Red Crescent Societies; the Ford Foundation; the Norwegian Agency for Development Cooperation; the Red Cross organizations of Norway, Germany, the U.S., Denmark, Sweden, and Spain; and a number of Japanese organizations.

18. Marita Sturken, *Tangled Memories: The Vietnam War, the AIDS Epidemic, and the Politics of Remembering* (Berkeley: University of California Press, 1997), 82.

19. Blumenthal.

20. In comparison, just 0.0026 percent of Americans receive compensation. Put another way: 1 in 25 Vietnamese suffers from AO; 1 in 38,564 Americans. Vietnamese Victims of Agent Orange, home page, http://www.vava.org.vn/; Stanley Kutler, *The Encyclopedia of the Vietnam War* (New York: Scribners, 1996), 111–16; CIA, "Vietnam," *The World Factbook*, https://www.cia.gov/ library/publications/the-world-factbook/geos/vm.html.

A CHILD, A MAN

Late in the afternoon, Tu rode his bicycle home slowly, enjoying the golden light. With his three children gone to the countryside to live with their grandmother for the summer, Tu felt like a free man. He pushed the bicycle up the rear steps to the kitchen of his top-floor apartment, and when he heard his wife speaking with someone in the apartment's front room, he quietly remained in the back to keep from interrupting.

Having two rooms was lucky. Either he or his wife could entertain a guest without disturbing the other. Out of courtesy, he would usually greet his wife's visitors, then return to the back, minding his own business. This was their ordinary way. But this time, when he peered into the front room, Tu simply nodded quietly to Loan. Her guest was a young boy, about thirteen or fourteen years old, and the fact that they sat conversing in front of a table spread with bowls of rice and dinner foods struck Tu as completely out of the ordinary. Silently, he retreated from the doorway to listen unobserved by the boy.

"Eat more, child, okay?" urged his wife. "Here, take more of this." She used her chopsticks to lever a chunk of fish into his bowl.

"Thank you, Auntie," said the boy sincerely. "To tell you the truth, Auntie, I eat a lot. In the past, I once ate seven bowls of rice."

"You're bragging!" laughed his wife. "When could you eat so much?"

"When my mother still lived with my father," said the boy. "My mother is really very kind, Auntie. And I'm not just saying that because she's my mother. The whole neighborhood says she's a kind and righteous woman. If anyone has a hard time, no matter who they are, my mother helps them. She really loves people."

Once again, Tu peeked into the room. Who was the boy's family, where was he from, and how had he come to speak so much like an adult?

Loan took the bowl, filled it with rice and returned it to the boy. He received it respectfully, taking it in both hands and saying meekly, "Thank you, Auntie," before taking a bit of the rice into his mouth and chewing thoughtfully.

"Have a taste of fried egg," suggested Loan.

"I don't like eggs," he said, "but I like eggplant very much. My mother knew how to preserve eggplant in salt with garlic and red ginger. But she never allowed me to eat too many because they're not good for you. And now . . . well, we never have eggplant to eat."

"Ah!" Loan smacked her lips. "Life is so hard now. There was a day when you could buy five eggplants with just one dong. Your father and stepmother have to ration, you understand."

The boy craned his thin neck while swallowing and opened his eyes wide. "Of course," he said, "I understand that, and I also know my father isn't truly a wicked person—he simply lacks discipline and heart."

"Why do you say that?"

Catching his carelessness, the boy lowered his head and changed the subject. "For sure, Auntie, I know how to think. We shouldn't expect too much from other people. Justice is founded on reason. At mealtimes, my stepmother gives eggs and meat to my half brother and sister, but to me she gives only a bowl of vegetables. I can see that's right. They are little, the younger one is three and the other six. I'm healthy as an elephant, and they're as little as cats, so how could I take their food?"

The boy laughed hollowly. "But sometimes my stepmother does strange things, Auntie. Yesterday, after work, my father brought home a box of powdered milk and made me a cup. It's been five or six years since I've seen any milk at all. But, I didn't get to drink it because she yanked the cup from me and threw it into the yard."

"My god!"

"It's true. Every day, that witch seems more and more wicked. She promised me if I don't collect enough vegetables for the rabbits each day she'll send me to sleep outside in the yard without my supper. She actually did that to me once, and I was so hungry my father secretly brought me a bowl of cold rice. But she knew. She ran out, grabbed the bowl from his hand and threw the rice to the ground. She said she'd rather give it to the dog than to me. Now I know better: I don't eat anything without her permission.

"You know, when her babies were small, my job was to carry them everywhere for her. She hadn't started to cut my rations yet, but even then she would always clench her teeth and say to me: 'Drop my baby and I'll kill you.' Just speaking those words out loud, I'm still scared. And I would never have dropped those babies, I love them so much. They were so sick all the time, and because I took care of them, I had to repeat sixth grade. Now I'm a big kid and still in the seventh grade, which sometimes makes me not want to go to school anymore."

The boy paused, a slightly amused and knowing smile on his lips. Then he said softly:

"Auntie, I could never be a wicked person, truly. When I see crippled people, I really feel pity for them. When I have some money in my pocket, I always give a penny to the blind street musician and his son on the streetcar. But the time I gave a beggar woman and her son two bowls of rice, my stepmother punished me, bashing my head against the wall, giving me a big lump. The other day I saw an old woman carrying heavy loads of rice on her shoulders to the railway station. I carried them for her, and even though she tried to give me ten dong, I wouldn't take her money. I had to take pity on such a poor old lady, right, Auntie?"

The boy's incredible story took Tu's breath away, drawing him into the room to get another look at the little speaker so adeptly discussing not only his personal feelings but also his family and his relation to society as well. His body looked stunted by malnutrition. He had a shriveled and suntanned face, but wide, sparkling eyes, smooth and black hair, pink, round ears, and an honest and open smile that charmed Tu into not really seeing his shortcomings. The boy combined two opposite characters: he had an experienced and clever mind thanks to his miserable life, but at the same time he was full of vitality, joy, and the love of life.

As an excuse to enter the room, Tu hung up his raincoat and said, "Why not set the food tray on the table, dear, so that our visitor can take his meal nicely?"

The boy started at Tu's voice, turning quickly to see him before murmuring a greeting. Abruptly, he set the bowl on the tray and stood up.

"I'm so full! Begging your permission, I'll go now."

"Please," said Tu amicably, "be our guest, stay and visit a while."

The boy smiled and shook his head, declining the cup of tea Loan poured for him. He politely bade them farewell and disappeared out the door.

Tu picked up the food tray and set it on the table.

Loan said, "I set it on the table, but the boy moved it to the floor."

"How did you meet him?"

"He saw me carrying the water up here and insisted on helping. Then he came into the room and played with the kids' toys: the doll, the little car, and the tank. He told me he's Mr. Thong's son, from one of the rear apartments. His father's an employee of a commercial company, and his stepmother, Sim, butchers meat at the state grocery. Kiem is the son of Thong's ex-wife. That's the problem. The big people have committed a crime against the small."

This last phrase of Loan's stunned them both into a silence that lasted through dinner and for the rest of the night.

From that day on, Kiem became a regular visitor at Tu and Loan's house. The boy needed to open his heart to someone, and since Loan was near retirement and her children were still living in the country for the summer, she had plenty of free time to give him. She genuinely enjoyed their simple conversations since she herself came from the countryside, and her face and thinking still bore traces of that simple life. And of course by nature she was very kind and honest.

The boy usually came in the afternoons. Occasionally he took dinner with them, but most of the time he didn't. When he could, Kiem gave them a bunch of fresh spinach that he himself had grown, telling them he wanted to share the fruit of his labor, which was more than enough for his family. Too frequently he sat on a chair looking very sad and tired, his face battered black and blue. He would help Loan peel peanut shells, winnow rice, or clean the floors, and he liked to talk while working, telling her the many things he happened to know or to have witnessed. For example, a woman from the house next door had compelled her stepdaughter to marry a man she didn't love, which prompted her to resist by committing suicide; the police had recently arrested an employee who worked for the state grocery; a nearby restaurant had been caught serving its customers counterfeit coffee. He could recite for Loan the names of many thieves, burglars, and smugglers. He also knew about the corruption of the officials who issued illegal documents to people fleeing the country and who accepted bribes to hire state company employees. Of course, he also spoke frequently about his family.

One day, while Loan emptied bags of purchased rice into her storage bin, he said, "Last week, my stepmother went to the pagoda, so I had a chance to visit my mother."

"Oh?" said Loan. "Where does your mother live?"

"Near Giap Bat Station," said the boy. He took some money from his shirt pocket and gave it to Loan. "She gave me thirty dong, and I'd like you to keep it for me so I won't be tempted to spend it all buying sweets. My mother already gave me a sticky rice cake and made me eat it right away so I wouldn't take it home and share it with my brother and sister."

"Your mother loves her own child best."

"I know, but I also love them very much."

"Kiem, your mother loves you so much, why don't you go back and live with her?"

"How could I, Auntie?" He opened his eyes wide, as if the question frightened him. "My mother has to keep everything she gives me a secret from her husband, even when it's something small, like that money or rice cake. He's rich, but wicked. He's a tanker truck driver. You know the saying, 'Tanker truck first, then bus, lorry third, and cars are always there,' so my stepfather is number one, the richest. When my mother married him, he made her cut all ties with me. Some big people are so small-minded! I visit my mother because I miss her, not because I want anything from her, but he always looks angry and suspicious when he sees me." Kiem paused. He turned his face to the door and seemed to be very sad. "But I don't blame either of them. They have had an ill-fated marriage. When my mother found out about my father's affair with the witch, she was so sad she wandered the streets all the time, and that's how they met. Adults are really complicated, Auntie! Too few of them dare to take money lightly."

Once again Tu marveled at the boy's perception. Seeing him off in the corridor, Tu pondered the boy's critique of adults and society, his hatred of the selfishness and wickedness he'd seen in his life. Tu breathed a sigh, thinking about the boy's ragged clothing.

A person's clothes establish his dignity and personality. With the uniform of a soldier, a person's whole attitude transforms and becomes self-confident. In this way, a thing is a way of the world, manifesting its owner's grown-up character. But with nothing, how would Kiem go into life, and what sort of person would he become?

The fate of the next generation is the eternal concern of all human beings. Are children a source of joy or the consequence of their parents' faults? Are they the blossoms on the trees or awkward bundles of firewood, so heavy and so difficult to carry? Human action—whether selfish indulgence or the struggle for a better life—can cause the breakdown of the family and create outcast children. The kids themselves experience bitterness and pain when people will not treat them well simply because they are not family. The situation gets even worse when those kids grow up because they treat the next generation with the same vehemence and brutality.

Tu's fears for the boy finally came true. After work one evening, as Tu carried his bicycle up the stairs to the apartment, Loan met him in the corridor, panic-stricken.

"Kiem has run away."

Tu's bicycle clattered against the wall and floor. He took a deep breath. "When did he leave?"

"He came at noon to ask me for the money I was keeping for him. I had to beg him to tell me where he planned to go, and finally he said he was going to Lao Cai to work in the apatite mines."

Tu lowered himself into a chair. "What happened?"

"His wicked stepmother . . ." Loan's eyes flooded with tears. "The neighbors are all saying it was terrible! Kiem accidentally broke a cup handle, and in retaliation his stepmother threw the broken cup at his face and nearly poked his eye out. People are saying she even forced him to kneel with his mouth crammed full of excrement. At the neighborhood meeting yesterday, some people criticized her for treating her stepson so cruelly. She came home so angry she made her husband tie Kiem to the bed and then beat him within an inch of his life. My god, what a brutal woman! How can such a nice and lovely boy endure such torture?"

Tu tried to keep calm, asking, "How do you know he's gone already?"

"He told me so. He said he'd been planning to leave for a long time but stayed for his brother and sister. That woman's been sick a lot lately, and Kiem worried the kids would suffer without someone to take care of them."

"Why didn't you stop him?"

"How could I stop him?" she cried, sobbing. "He said he had made up his mind. I gave him some rice to eat and made him take twenty thousand dong. He thanked me and sent his best regards to you and then left for the train station on foot."

Tu felt as if a very precious thing had fallen from his hand. He sat silently, the belief that he had some responsibility in the boy's story weighing heavily on his heart. He had never found another path for the boy, never done anything to really help him or warn Kiem's father and stepmother to treat him better. Lately, Kiem's problems had become an obsession, keeping him awake at night thinking of them. Tu and his wife were simple, ordinary people, not rich or powerful, but they loved each other and their three children very much, providing them with a moral and affectionate environment in which they could grow up to be good people. Kiem had run away! Where could he be now? Smugglers, thieves, and burglars could be anywhere, and Kiem could easily fall victim to them or even be enticed to join them if he didn't know what else to do. The boy was still too young to make his way in the world.

After sitting quietly in a chair for a long while, Tu said, "Why don't we adopt the boy, or at least take him to the country to live with my parents?"

Loan did not turn around. She looked through the window, its light accentuating her thin face. Her smooth eyelashes vibrated while she spoke: "I've thought the same and even told him we might be able to adopt him. He thanked me but said it wouldn't work, that his stepmother would complicate it all, denouncing the family throughout the neighborhood, saying we'd interfered with him, encouraging him to be worse."

Tu stood up, beating his hand on the chair. "What does it mean to interfere? I have a right to love the boy, a responsibility to protect kids, no matter whose they are. The law doesn't give a stepmother permission to torture her stepchild. I'm going to write an article to denounce her."

Loan smacked her lips. "That woman is a beast."

Beast!

The word made sense. It captured her deceit, her neglect, and her brutality based on blind instinct. If she were only selfish and calculating, she wouldn't treat the boy so badly. Even a calculating merchant, caring not a whit for justice or humanity, would know a good profit could be made by feeding the boy since he took care of the children, grew vegetables, kept rabbits and chickens, cleaned the house and cooked for the family. Not to mention the fact that he did all those things well. He provided her with much more than she invested in him.

Thus, it could only be this woman's instinctive brutality, her unjust, blind, and selfish nature that aroused her hatred for everyone not tied by blood to her.

Tu wanted his article to make people see her wickedness as a threat to the health of the whole community. To gather material, one day he went to the state grocery to see how his subject ran her business.

Sim was about thirty-five. Sharp-witted and glib, she also had quick hands for slicing, weighing, and wrapping the meats. While doing everything, she constantly shifted her eyes here and there, her thin lips chattering out words like bursts of machine-gun fire. Such a strong voice would seem to belong to a healthy body, full of vitality, but Sim's skinny body seemed barely capable of containing it. A gold necklace sparkling between her breasts drew attention to how flat they were. Her high cheekbones made her face look thin. Only her smooth, black eyebrows remained to suggest the beauty that must have attracted Kiem's father in the first place. In fact, her sunken eyes and papery skin gave away just how seriously her illness had affected her health.

Despite himself, Tu pitied her. She was so sick! Maybe sick enough to distort her character and temperament, to compel her to act so horribly. Was writing the denouncement necessary? Should she be forgiven?

A bulky woman shoved to the counter in front of him, took a big piece of meat and put it in her plastic bag. Obviously, she had some special relationship with Sim because instead of paying she simply smiled and said in a friendly way, "Did that little bastard really go?"

The stepmother took up a pig's foot and bashed the snout.

"Like crap into pants."

"Did he steal anything?"

"If he did, I'll beat him to a pulp."

Tu no longer felt pity, hearing her speak this way.

He went straight to the local People's Committee office. A woman working there confirmed Tu's estimate of Sim's character, mentioning her wicked treatment of her husband's son and the complaints of corruption from many of her customers.

Outrage fueled Tu's writing and he finished his article quickly. Two weeks later, it was published with a title meant to provoke anger from the readers: Preventing the torture of a husband's child. It included an abbreviated form of Sim's name and address, and presented the author as "The Builder."

Two days after publication, Tu was sitting in his room when a roar bellowed in from the apartment courtyard. He came to the window and immediately recognized the subject of his article.

Though thin and sickly, the stepmother had come as herself, not the employee of a state-run company, letting loose with all her ferocious cruelty. Seeing her fury, Tu imagined how the boy had suffered.

Her freckled face boiled crimson. She stood defiantly akimbo. She craned her neck and a small tuft of her hair hung at the back of her neck. From her mouth came a nonstop string of curses that she punctuated with her feet, tramping her seven-inch wooden heels into the dirt.

"Damn you, you rotten bastard. You dirty slanderer! You encouraged the little shit to break up my family!" She began counting his offenses on her fingers, holding them out in accusation. "You're trammeling my reputation as a good state employee! You're an imperialist betraying our country! You're as brutal as the Khmer Rouge, as Pol Pot! God will not forgive you for your crimes. I fed this little shit when he was a baby and he ate double the food I fed my own children. He repaid me with ingratitude and theft. That's right! Three taels of gold and five hundred dong."

Sim clenched her fingers and shook her fist, staring at Tu in the window and letting fly with another staccato burst of her machine gun mouth. She wanted revenge.

Just as Tu began to feel like anything could happen next, the man who must have been her husband stepped up behind her. He had a thick beard, sulky eyes, and ponderous body. He said something to her in a low voice and immediately Sim shoved his face away and said:

"Damn it! Leave me alone. I have to fight his slanderous lies. That bastard accused me of stealing another woman's husband and torturing my stepson. That hypocrite pretended to feel pity for the little shit. I dare him to have a debate right now. If he's too chicken to come out and talk, let him talk to himself in the shitter."

Voices and laughter clattered down to them from the apartment balconies, where people had crowded the corridors, watching and enjoying the spectacle like it was a comedic performance.

Loan left the corridor for the room and said angrily, "What a cruel woman! Doesn't she know curses come back to curse?"

Curses come back to curse! Could the folk saying be true?

Tu didn't believe in mysterious, supernatural forces ruling over human fate. But Tu took pause when he returned home from his office one day to find an ambulance just arriving. A crowd had gathered, and after the fuss around the ambulance, people began to explain that Sim had collapsed climbing the stairs.

Calmly aloof from the scene, Tu pondered the variability of human fate. For many days after that, it seemed neither Tu nor Loan wanted to raise the devil speaking of that horrible woman.

Detached, as if it cared for nothing, time drifted on.

One day, Tu was resting at home when a knock disturbed him. Opening the door, Tu was shocked to find Kiem, the miserable little boy, still too small for his age but with the same smart and sparkling eyes that seemed old beyond his years, standing there, holding the hands of a little girl and a little boy. He admonished them, "Chi and Oanh, say hello to Mr. Tu, will you?" And then Kiem smiled broadly and said himself, "Hello, Uncle!"

Loan came out from the back room astonished, saying happily, "Is this Kiem? Where have you come from? When did you arrive?"

"Come in, come in!" said Tu with great warmth, ushering in his little guests.

Kiem raised his eyes, revealing them to be wet with tears.

"I came home just yesterday. I had to come and see you to say hello, but soon we need to go to the hospital to see my stepmother."

"Where have you been?" asked Loan anxiously.

"Ms. Hoa, my cousin who graduated from chemistry school, works at Cam Duong apatite mine in Lao Cai. She brought me there and lets me study at the primary school for the mine workers' children. I also work part-time at the mine. Eventually, I'll go to a vocational school. I've met many kind people up there. . . . I just came home because I found out about my stepmother being taken to the hospital and because no one's taking care of my poor brother and sister. My father is so sad he doesn't do anything. And I think my stepmother has had a very difficult time with this bout of illness." After a short pause, he lowered his head and wiped his tears before continuing in a voice choked with emotion. "She has liver cancer, you know, with almost no chance to survive. She was exposed to Agent Orange during the war when she worked on the Ho Chi Minh Trail as a member of the volunteer youth corps."

"My god!" Loan exclaimed, taking the boy's hand.

Stunned by Kiem's account of his stepmother, Tu suddenly felt pity for her again. The boy's eyes were full of tears too.

"I think my stepmother's been sick a long time. Maybe she's really not a bad person. She volunteered to go to the war at eighteen. She lived and worked in a forest where American planes sprayed their deadly toxic chemicals, withering the grass, stripping the leaves, and killing all the trees. The streams and even the ground dried up. They had to squeeze rotten leaves just to have some water to cook their meals. Dear Uncle and Auntie, now I can only feel pity for my stepmother."

Unable to restrain himself, Tu hugged the boy, letting his love pour out. Kiem willingly came home to share the pain and distress of his stepmother. He took no joy in her suffering, even though she herself had caused him so much pain. His attitude, speech, tone, and accent were full of love and sorrow for the unhappy woman, whom he treated as his own flesh and blood. Kiem was a strong, promising, and hopeful seed of human nature, having come into being naively and naturally but now also needing to be protected, cultivated, and encouraged to grow.

Tu sat quietly in the armchair for a long time after Kiem and the children left, trying to get a grip on himself after his mind and heart had been overwhelmed by such strange thoughts and feelings. Tu loved and believed in the pure heart and energy of the boy. He hoped a great spirit and impenetrable dignity might emerge from such misery. But one worry still plagued him: how could that woman ever recover from such an illness?

Hanoi, 1984

TRANSLATED BY HUY LIEN AND CHARLES WAUGH

THIRTEEN HARBORS

I took a new wife for my husband.

Maybe the strangest thing ever to happen at Yen Ha village, I chose my good friend to be the bride, a woman who had passed the age for marriage but for a long time had desired a child and wanted a husband. Besides making the match, I helped my husband's sister and mother during the engagement ceremony and wedding, preparing dishes for their celebration.

Of course, for the others, the wedding had its share of happiness, but for me it held only humiliation and sorrow. Just at the moment when my husband took his new bride to the bedroom, I slipped silently through the back door and into the garden. Bag in hand, I wept while walking the road down to the river. I called for a ferry and crossed back to my mother's home.

There is a saying, *A girl has twelve harbors*, meaning only at the last will she find shelter. It took me thirteen.

2

I had gone into labor the first time at noon.

It was the fifth lunar month, and the harvest was nearly finished. I had brought rice and corn and sweet potatoes to the harvesters in the field. Grasshoppers swarmed over the paddy, their wings clacking and sputtering. The harvesters had to throw down their sickles and chase after them. Kicking through the stubble, I waded into the paddy too. Suddenly I had a pain in my belly that very rapidly became worse and worse. I threw my grasshoppers into my hat and held my belly. My water broke, soaking my trousers before I reached the field's edge. I called to my husband. Bewildered, he dropped the unfinished sheaf of rice plants from his hands, ran over and lowered me in his arms to the ground. My mother-in-law nearly lost her head sending our nephew for a midwife. But it was too late. I gave birth right there on the wet earth, surrounded by the new rice plants on one side and the stubble of the old on the other.

"There's so much . . . the earth is soaked . . . oh!" cried my mother-in-law.

Terrified by my mother-in-law's mournful cry, I raised my head to look at my belly, and nearly fainted when I saw what I had given birth to: instead of a baby, just a piece of bloody, red meat. It had a dark mouth that looked like a fish running aground and yawning before dying. The mud-spattered harvesters gathered round, splashing and tramping in from all over the field.

"Put it in a pot and bury it in the Serpent Mound," said someone.

"No, put it on a banana tree raft and float it down the river," said another.

After this, I didn't leave the house and cried all the time, my silent husband looking after me as carefully as a little child. Tears brimmed in my mother-in-law's eyes when she looked at my emaciated face. She treated me like her own daughter.

One day, I asked her sadly, "Mother, how have I come to this?"

She breathed a sigh and said, "All the members of our family are kind-hearted people. We did not sow the breeze that resulted in this whirlwind on your body."

Just then, my husband accidentally dropped a pot of medicine. The pot broke and the wet yellow medicine plopped all over the floor, its steam rising.

I lost sleep frequently. Sometimes in my dreams I saw the harvesters wearing conical hats, sitting on the lawn and smoking tobacco while waiting for that piece of meat to stop yawning. After a while they put it in a terracotta pot. Then they took it to the Serpent Mound and buried it. Sometimes I had another dream in which they put my piece of red meat on a banana tree raft and floated it down the Hoang Long. Then a serpent monster with long black hair would surface from the depths and push the raft back to the riverbank. After either of these dreams I would wake with a start, yelling, "Give back my baby! Give me my baby!"

Opening my eyes, I'd find my husband holding me in his arms, my body cold with sweat. He held me this way through many nightmares.

3

During the summer of the year of the rooster, there was little rain in our village, but the water roared in from upstream for a whole week, catching my village in a heavy flood. The river flowed full of big logs and branches. The dike broke at midnight, releasing a thunderous swell. Dogs howled, and the chickens clucked madly, inciting the cows and buffaloes and goats to bawl and break down the gates of their stables. Panicky villagers ran here and there seeking safety. Just as I climbed to the top of a banyan tree, the river swallowed the village. I sat in the tree for hours, calling in the dim moonlight for my mother, terrified the serpent monster would come and drown me. Under the pull of the water, the banyan first began to lean, then uprooted and washed away. Hungry and exhausted, I was swept away by the flood.

I awoke the next morning to find myself sprawled on the Serpent Mound. Many villagers had gathered there, some standing, some sitting on their heels. The floodwaters moiled all around us.

A dog was barking. My mother-in-law looked at me sadly, surprising me when she said: "It was the serpent monster that saved you and brought you to the mound."

At sixteen, I had met a team of archaeology students who came to my village to excavate the Serpent Mound. I knew one of the students, a boy named Tao, who had also grown up in Yen Ha village. He seemed to sympathize with me and liked to tease me. They excavated all week without finding anything but the shells of mussels and shipworms, animal bones, and a wooden plank. Before replacing the dirt, Tao threw a straw doll into the pit.

"It's magic to use against any girl who might love and then betray me," he said. "It will turn the traitor into a serpent monster."

All the students laughed while I blushed with shame and bewilderment. Later, when we fell in love with each other, I asked him about the straw doll, but he wouldn't answer except with an enigmatic smile.

Despite the students' failure to turn anything up, stories about the mound persisted. One had it that during a moonlit night, a dense mist covered the river. The waves popped and echoed from a cave carved by the river in a limestone karst. A thief returning home in the dark could not find a ferry, so he began to remove his clothes, intending to carry them across on his head with the things he had stolen. Just then, a fishing boat glided silently to the riverbank. A boatgirl whose ragged shirt exposed her breast sat at the rudder.

"Come aboard," she said. "I'll take you across."

The thief climbed into the boat and, thinking indecent thoughts, happily found no one else aboard. When they reached the middle of the river, he advanced on the girl. Without hesitation, she slipped over the edge of the boat into the water, where he saw that only the upper part of her body appeared to be human. The lower half tapered into the long, wriggling tail of a serpent. Horror welled up inside him as he realized he had just embraced a serpent monster. Dumbfounded, he watched the head, bare shoulders, and breasts of the girl emerge from the water. With both hands on the bow, she tipped the boat to let the water rush in, sinking it immediately. The thief could have drowned, but fortunately the current pushed him to shore instead. Trembling, he scrambled up the bank, but the serpent monster called him back: "Don't go! You forgot your bag."

When he turned, he found the girl as he first saw her. Her dry trouser cuffs had been rolled up around her thighs, revealing pale, human legs. She stood in the boat at the river's edge, holding the bag out to him, its many stolen things and the bag itself all completely dry. She let the bag drop to shore, then rowed into the mist and disappeared. After that night, obsessed with those events, the thief suffered from bouts of madness for half a year.

But to me, half a year is nothing: all my young life has been haunted by the serpent monster and the misty harbor.

4

My husband's name was Lang. As a soldier bound for the front, he received a few weeks of leave before going to war. At first he didn't want to get married. Instead, he spent most of his time wandering around the village visiting relatives and friends, laughing and joking and drinking as if he would not return. When the leave was nearly finished, under great pressure from his mother, he hastened to find a woman who would agree to marry him. I met him while still grieving for Tao, who I'd heard had died at the front.

As a bride I was taken to my husband's house by boat. While the wedding party went ashore, I dipped water into a large gourd jar. According to village custom, this water would be used to wash the feet of my husband's mother. I don't know when the custom became popular in these villages, but people say it helps to prevent the fatal rivalry between mothers- and daughters-in-law, and I think they might be right. Before the wedding, my mother gave me the dry gourd jar along with instructions for acting and working as a good daughter-in-law.

Of course at that time, I knew the saying, *A girl has twelve harbors*, but I didn't yet know how many I would have to pass.

The wedding procession climbed slowly up the hill to where a large crowd had gathered and was shouting angrily. Suddenly I recognized Tao, my former lover, in the middle with a whitewashed flat basket hung around his neck that said, "I am a deserter." I couldn't believe the man burdened with that flat basket was my lover. When all the areas in the north had been overwhelmed by American bombing, most schools had closed, and Tao joined the army. It had been reported that he had died in a battle on the front line. But now the rumor running through the crowd had him so afraid of battle that he shot himself in the foot. Court-martialled, he had been sent home to be reeducated, which now appeared to mean being paraded around the village by a group of militiamen who condemned him as a deserter and traitor to his country. Tao limped ahead, followed by the militiamen carrying their AK-47s on their shoulders, urging him to call out: "I am a coward! I betrayed my country!" Many kids followed them, jeering and repeating in unison: "I am a coward! I betrayed my country!"

Walking by the side of my husband, feeling such a pang in my heart, I did not know what to say.

One day after the wedding, Lang left for the front. We had no idea how long it would be before we met each other again. He tried to hide his sorrow, rushing through his farewells and leaving the village quickly.

5

During the war, a woman suffered terribly living without her husband. Many endless and sleepless nights I lay on the bed, longing for a kiss or an embrace. Heart-broken, I would cover my face with his old shirt. I suffered much more just before my time of the month, when my breasts would swell with a slight pain and my cheeks turn pink, my eyes glittering with desire.

During those long nights, many things happened in my imagination. When I smelled his shirt, it seemed I could smell the faint odor of his breath as well. But this only worked for a short while. To distract myself, I had to put paddy into the grinder and husk rice all night long. Sometimes I went to the well and ceaselessly poured buckets of cold water over my body, and sometimes I would go to my mother-in-law's bed and lie by her side because her breath was similar to my husband's.

Since my mother-in-law had her own experience of the days waiting for her husband from the front, she knew how I felt and thought she could help me. She put Lang's underwear in a pan and simmered them over a low flame, stirring them with a stick while murmuring her prayers. She believed this ritual helped a daughter-in-law be faithful to a husband far away.

Yen Ha village had two places along the riverside where villagers usually came to bathe: one upstream for women, the other, some two hundred meters downstream, for men. The women usually waded into the river without taking off their clothes. Away from the bank where the water rose high to their chests, they would roll their shirts to their heads like turbans and swim and wash themselves.

One of my many troubles came from bathing at this river. On a hot day while walking with his men along the riverside, the chief of the militia discovered Tao and me swimming together. The chief bitterly hated draft dodgers and deserters. It galled him to believe these cowards seemed to have the time and opportunity to flirt with the wives of the soldiers fighting on the front lines. Of course he felt so strongly about it because his own wife had been caught having an affair with a ferry-boat worker and later became pregnant. As a result, he often spied on the women who talked with the workers at the riverside.

"I had a cramp," I insisted to the chief. "This man saved me from drowning."

Frightened, Tao stammered, "I heard her … cry for help when I … when I brought my … buffalo cart … to the river."

The militiamen wanted to take me and Tao to the Commune Administration, where they would interrogate us about our relationship. Tao wore only pants and walked lamely behind me. My black silk trousers clung wetly to my skin. I hadn't had time to put on my blouse, so I had just a camisole on my upper body. Suddenly, the chief told me to stop and put on my blouse. He changed his mind about the interrogation and sent me home.

"I'm letting you go," he said, "not because you deserve it, but out of consideration for the man at the front."

Nevertheless, as I walked away, I heard him cursing me behind my back, complaining about "faithless women."

6

When the war ended, my husband came home. Seeing him return whole and unharmed loosed a flood of happiness, both in me as well as the rest of the family. But Lang became peevish just a few days later. The incident at the river had made me notorious in the village, and I had no idea how to explain my relationship with Tao to him. One evening, a host of friends and relatives came to our house, celebrating Lang's return as merrily as if it were Tet. But after they left, a funeral gloom settled on our home.

Sensing the cause of his mood, my mother-in-law said to Lang, "I'm sorry for not having been able to keep a good reputation for your wife."

"I survived the war for many years," said Lang, "only to have this bad reputation kill me now."

Coldly, I said, "I am your wife. Only you can know whether I've been faithful or not."

Embarrassed and surprised, Lang mulled over what I had said. He could not decide whether to make our marriage work or to divorce me. As a soldier who had been far away from home for such a long time, it was difficult for him to know his own heart.

One night shortly thereafter, during a windy and very cool full moon, no one in the village could sleep. Nearly everyone gathered outside to enjoy the moonlight sparkling between the fishing boats anchored on the Hoang Long. But Lang and I stayed inside, lying on the bed and listening to the continuous clatter echoing back from the river where the fishermen knocked oars against their hulls to attract fish. When Lang's hand accidentally brushed against my body, I took it in my own. With this one touch, everything changed and we embraced each other passionately.

My mother-in-law got up early the next morning. She sat on the verandah, combing her hair and looking toward our bedroom now and then. When Lang stepped from our room, he sat by her side.

"Luckily, I kept my patience these past few days," he said. "If not, I might have murdered that bastard deserter, Tao, and ruined my marriage."

"What do you mean?" asked his mother.

"The one night after my marriage before I left for the war was Sao's time of the month," said Lang. "We just held each other and wept."

"Do you mean your wife is still a virgin?"

"Yes, until last night."

My mother-in-law was embarrassed and sat quietly. I stepped from the bedroom and rolled my hair with my hands. When gazing at myself in the mirror, I found my eyes bright and flowing with happiness. Then I sat by her side with a light heart.

"I didn't believe the rumor about you," she said. "But we had no witness to restore your reputation until now. Forgive me and don't be angry with me for what I've allowed to happen to you."

I laid my hand on her arm. "I am not angry with anyone. And I've never been afraid of anything, except that the war would prevent my husband from coming home. Only he could truly know how I've longed for his return."

7

I gave birth to pieces of red meat at the end of my second, third, and fourth pregnancies. Frightened and sad, my mother-in-law spent most of her time praying to the Buddha. But Buddha never came to help us. People say *A wife's one hundred joys are not her husband's debts*, but all the members of my husband's family were virtuous, and yet I still had to bear this burden. Where did it come from?

I would not have thought it possible, but my womb produced even greater terrors during my fifth pregnancy. Several round balls of red meat emerged this time, like the red, leathery eggs a serpent monster might lay. But neither human nor devil would hatch from what I had carried for so many months and with so much pain.

Some villagers began to despise and shun me. One day, a pack of kids followed me, shouting, "Crazy woman! Crazy woman!"

Later my husband told me about the things I couldn't remember doing. I lost many hours wandering along the side of the Hoang Long river, slipping into the water, taking wild flowers and scattering them on the shore. Apparently I did this many times. Once I went to the Serpent Mound, where many small memorials had been raised for all the village's dead children. But I didn't know which ones belonged to my pieces of red meat.

8

One night the river ran low, and my husband and I went shrimping. Boat lamps sparkled all over the water, and the shrimp eyes reflecting the light became innumerable red dots glittering just beneath the surface. Once we had cast the net on the river, Lang pitched a tent for us on the Serpent Mound. If there were very few shrimp or fish to catch, we would sleep in the tent until morning. But this night, after catching half a basket of shrimp, I became tired and went to the tent to rest. Some time in the night I heard a woman call: "Give back my baby!"

A woman stepped down from the top of the mound, shouting: "They drowned my baby at the river. Help me! Give back my baby!"

"Are you crazy?" I told her. "You don't have a baby, you never . . ."

"Yes, I do," she interrupted. "That's my baby! Don't drown my baby, please."

I looked to where she pointed on the river and saw Tao putting pieces of red meat on a banana tree raft. The woman jumped down from the riverbank into the water. Then a serpent with a girl's upper body and long black hair rose to the surface and pushed the raft to shore. My heart filled with terror and I looked around, but Tao and the raft had disappeared. Only a flock of wild white ducks flew low over the river, quacking.

"Sao! Sao!" Lang clapped my shoulders. "Are you okay?"

"It was Mrs. Sao who called for help," I said, still not fully conscious. "It was Mrs. Sao who jumped down the river and turned into the serpent."

"Are you out of your mind? You are Sao, my wife." His eyes searched my own. "Let's go to the river, let's cast the net."

And so we cast the net until dawn.

On the way to the market to sell the shrimp, I met Tao, who carried terracotta pots in his buffalo cart.

"I hate those pots, Tao," I said. "They look terrible. Stop carrying them in your cart."

"Okay, but why do you hate them so much?"

I told him about my nightmare and said, "Do you remember when you came with the students to excavate the Serpent Mound, and you buried a straw doll in the pit? Why did you do that?"

Tao laughed. "It made no sense. I was just teasing. But the straw doll legend is real, from the war between Vietnam and the Cham, who lived here many centuries ago. Under the reign of Tran Nghe Tong, the Cham navy came up the Hoang Long river from the sea, killing many people and burning the villages along the river. But strangely, they did nothing to Yen Ha village. When Tran Khat Chan, the Vietnamese general, defeated Che Bong Nga, the Cham general, the invaders fled to the sea. Only our village survived the war intact. But three months later, a lot of things became known more terrible than the fate of the villages destroyed by war. Scores of unmarried girls in our village turned out to be pregnant.

"The elders shaved the girls' heads and marked them with lime, then tied the girls to banana tree rafts and floated them down the river. But although the rafts floated downstream in the morning, by evening they had been pushed back to the village by hundreds of shrimp, fish, serpents, and turtles. The elders became angry and directed the young men in the village to push the rafts downstream, but again and again they came back. Finally, the villagers gave up and freed the poor girls from their punishment. Many months later these girls gave birth to curly-haired, dark-skinned, and wild-eyed children who didn't have the same flesh and blood as the villagers.

"Among those women, one gave birth to a piece of red meat with a round mouth that looked like a copper penny. Immediately, the villagers took the piece of red meat for a devil and floated it down the river. The young woman went mad, screaming incessantly: 'Give back my baby! Give me my baby!' At night, she went to the Hoang Long to look for her child. She waded into the river, swimming and diving all over, but could not find her baby. At last, exhausted, she slipped under the water and drowned. Then by some magic her body transformed into a serpent and washed ashore. The villagers buried the serpent body with copper pennies, tortoise shells, and a girl-shaped straw doll on an island in the middle of the river. They even built a tomb for her. That's how this place became the Serpent Mound. They hoped honoring her would help to prevent such a terrible thing from happening again. The legend says the woman's soul still wanders the river and caves it passes. When a person might drown in the river, the woman changes into a serpent and saves her life.

"To pray for that woman's soul, you should put a clod of earth on the mound. Have you?"

"No, we didn't know."

"That's too bad. You should do it now."

9

My husband and I walked the twelve kilometers into town to receive medical exams at the provincial hospital. The doctor told us: "Both of you are in good health and none of your test results explain Mrs. Sao's abnormal childbirths. We'd like you to visit a hospital in Hanoi if you can get there."

Lang told me to sell a cow at the market. His mother gave us a pair of earrings. Lang's younger sister gave us two breeding pigs, and my mother gave us a hundred kilos of paddy. We sold it all, except the earrings, which we planned to use to pay for medicine. "Nothing is more important than life," we thought. "If we have our health, we can make more money."

We went to the hospital in Hanoi and had at least ten different kinds of tests. The doctor finally said he could find nothing wrong with me, but he wanted to have a private talk with Lang and asked me to leave the room.

Afterward, Lang told me the doctor said the dioxin level in his blood was very high. He took him to a laboratory to see hundreds of glass jars containing various kinds of deformed fetuses. The doctor explained: "In some cases, soldiers affected by Agent Orange can still give birth to normal children, but who knows what will happen when their children have children, or when all this will end?"

After returning home, Lang lay quietly on the bed for three days. His face sagged with exhaustion, making him look much older than his age.

"My darling," he said finally, "I don't want to lie to you. The doctor thinks I've been affected by Agent Orange. He thinks if we keep trying to have children, we'll probably keep having these deformities."

"Agent Orange?" I exclaimed. "You must have known!"

"How could I know?" said Lang. "I feel fine. But after speaking with the doctor, I thought about the defoliated forests we had to cross. We drank water from streams running through them and even put some in our canteens. Once, in the jungle, we watched American planes flying slowly overhead spraying a dense white mist. A few days later, the leaves shriveled and came down easily in the breeze. All the trees withered and turned the color of death."

Wrapped in my husband's heart, I felt a pain there like one I'd not yet seen. Withered and bitter myself, I had no comfort to pour into him.

10

Lang received a letter from Ha Van Nenh, a former comrade, announcing that his new wife had just given birth to a son. Lang asked me to prepare some gifts for a visit to Nenh's family: a dozen eggs and several kilos of sticky rice.

Nenh's family lived in a stilt house built on a green hill in the mountains. When we arrived, the door was open, and the sound of a baby crying came from inside. A little girl with no arms and no hair on her red head stood by the stilts baring her teeth in a grin like a monkey. Afraid to be bitten, I hid behind my husband.

Surprised and pleased to see us, Nenh welcomed us to his home. Nenh's wife, Thuy, carried her baby in her arms and gave us a cheery hello.

"Your wife looks young and healthy," I told Nenh, and asked her to let me hold the baby.

"My first wife had three pregnancies," said Nenh, "but each produced deformities like you see with this one here. After her birth, my wife was so tired and frightened she abandoned us. Thuy is my new wife."

Suddenly during the conversation, Lang's face turned white. "Where did you get these water barrels?" he asked.

Nenh said after the war he had been assigned to a project building a veterans' cemetery. He and his friends had found many barrels scattered in the forest that they thought might be used for water. One of Nenh's comrades was a lorry driver and helped transport the barrels to their villages in the North.

"My god! What stupidity!" cried Lang. "You've brought death to your family. These defoliant containers are what deformed your children."

Nenh's face wrinkled and turned pale.

11

After returning home from Nenh's, Lang told his mother about Nenh's marrying a new wife who gave birth to a healthy son. After thinking it over for several days, Lang explained his decision for making a change in our lives: "A new marriage might bring us better luck. Who knows?"

Lang said he hoped if I married a healthy man, I might have normal children and a good family. Upset by Lang's proposal, I kept silent for many days.

One day when Lang was out, my mother-in-law came to my bedroom and asked, "What do you think for the future of your little family?"

"I have no idea," I said. I still didn't want to talk. But she was patient with me, despite my disrespectful tone.

"I am not so selfish as to think only of Lang," said my mother-in-law. "I have always treated you as my own daughter. I wish some change would be good for both of you."

"So you want me to leave my husband and allow him to marry a new wife," I said, crying. "But can you be sure his new wife will give birth to a healthy child?"

"No one could be sure of anything in such a situation," she said, "but let's try." Suddenly she knelt down to me. "My darling, I beg you to show mercy to Lang, to our family, and to yourself. You might have a better life with a healthy husband."

"Oh, Mother!" I said, taking her hands in mine. "I am grateful for your kindness and good will, but let me think carefully before I tell you what I feel we must do."

Sadly, I found myself clinging to the hope for a normal life and child and agreed with my mother-in-law to try again, repeating in my mind what Lang had said: "Who knows?"

12

After helping my husband marry a new wife, I went back to my own mother's home, where she took pity on me, weeping. Half a year passed. I couldn't forget the days and nights when Lang and I worked hard for our living, the smell of sweat from his shirt and face, the long days when I expected good or bad news of him from the front, or the long nights when we slept in the tent by the river and cast our nets for shrimp. Of course, neither could I forget my five terrible births.

I often went to the riverside at sunset and looked at my former husband's house, where the cook smoke rose from the thatch roof into the sky. Did he remember me when he slept with his new wife?

I knew the cause of my misfortune after visiting the hospital with Lang, but the straw doll Tao buried in the Serpent Mound still haunted me. One day I took a pick and shovel and crossed the river to the Serpent Mound. I dug for hours.

I had just begun to drag out a skeleton when Tao drifted by in his boat.

"Tao," I cried, "This is the serpent monster that destroyed my life."

"That's crazy," said Tao. "That story was just a joke."

"This isn't a skeleton of a serpent monster?"

"It's just some animal."

"Why did you lie to me? That serpent monster story has haunted me for so long."

"Forget the serpent monster," he said. "You have something more important to worry about."

I looked at him expectantly.

"Stay calm, okay? Lang's new wife has just given birth to eleven pieces of red meat."

I began to tremble.

"Sao, my darling…"

A ringing sounded in my ears. "Lang and me," I murmured, "it's hard to tell who's more miserable."

13

I had to cross the river again.

My friend could not bear the burden of my husband's house. After the miscarriage, she left quickly. Lang clenched his teeth and endured the disaster, even while his mother had become seriously ill. They needed my help more than ever, leaving me no choice but to try my thirteenth harbor.

I chose to cross at night. A dense mist covered the river, the ferry barely visible from the flickering of the boatgirl's cookfire. Once on board, I noticed the many terracotta pots inside the boat, and my limbs went limp with fear. When we reached the middle of the river, dozens of banana tree rafts began to bump into us, blocking our way. The boatgirl used her pole to repel the rafts. But after one raft had been pushed away, another came back again, swarming with the others all around. "We can't get through here," cried the boatgirl. "We have to turn back and cross somewhere else."

"This is the last harbor," I insisted. "We must cross here."

I helped the girl push the rafts away. Finally they dispersed, and the ferry crossed the river, my hardest crossing yet.

Once ashore, I turned to the river and found the banana tree rafts had vanished. The boat and the boatgirl sank into the mist, and the last thing I saw was the terracotta pots under the boat's dim light fading away.

Hanoi, 2004

TRANSLATED BY CHARLES WAUGH AND HUY LIEN

NGUYEN QUANG LAP

THE GOAT HORN BELL

It took more than half their lives just to meet each other again. Perhaps it was not uncommon. After a twenty-one gun salute, thousands of husbands and wives reunited after decades of separation. Husband in the North, wife in the South, husband in an American prison and wife waiting somewhere outside, from in the jungles and under the sea, now finally embracing in joy and sorrow. These reunions were fortunate; too frequently just one meter remained between couples, enough earth to keep them from ever embracing again.

He searched for her in Nha Trang and Phan Thiet and didn't find her. Outside of Da Nang, after ten days with no luck, hurriedly searching every place he thought she might be, finally he found her in the courtyard of the Minh Hieu military headquarters. She stood with several families in the yard, holding a two-year-old baby, whispering something to it. He stood transfixed at the gate, his chest pained as if pierced with needles. The day they parted so long ago, they had no child.

But he approached—step-by-step, slow and sure. Go ahead, there is nothing to fear, he told himself. This had been his motto for thirty-six years in the army. She didn't recognize him yet, thinking only, Here comes someone else to beg the committee for something, to wheedle, complain, or charge someone for something. He could see her clearly. She still appeared young, but, oh, so pale.

"Lanh!" he called softly.

She opened her eyes wide. Flustered, she set the child on the ground to toddle back to its mother, ran her fingers through her hair and stared at him.

He stooped suddenly and tightened his sandal straps. Damn, why am I doing this? He looked up.

"Oh God!" she whispered, recognizing him at last and crying into her hands. He ran to her, taking her into his arms. Suddenly she shoved him away, surprising him, and just as suddenly, she reconsidered: What's the matter! This is my husband, my Chi, who else? It was not easy to suspend her instincts for self-defense. In their twenty-one years apart she had not allowed herself to be embraced by anyone. Throwing herself into his chest, she sobbed, "My love! How long it was!"

The day they had parted he had promised her it would only be two years before they met again.

He took her to his home in his division's residential district. He had become a colonel, chief of staff for the division. She had spent those twenty-one years cooking at bases just behind the front lines. Within a day, all the cadres and soldiers in the division knew he had finally found her and came to congratulate them. Division Commander Hung, who had fought beside him for ten years, could not hold back his special feelings for them and came to visit ten consecutive evenings in a row. Once, after a long pause, the commander asked him, "Lanh can still . . . bear a child, can't she?" Chi smiled and said, "We think so . . . my wife is forty-six already . . . but we're going to try!" The commander shook him by the shoulders: "Good! Good!"

She felt she could still carry a child, but she was very weak. During her sixteen years in the jungle, she had been infected by chronic malaria, which paled her skin and thinned her hair. Every night, he held her in his arms, and she listened carefully to his heartbeat, each to be sure of the other's health. He was old too; fifty-seven. Many times when she gazed up at him, she wondered at the aged, war-torn face beside her. She would hug him, feel his dry and slippery back, the layer of dead cells thicker each day, and sigh, thinking if they did not have a child this next year, there would be no hope left. Only a few people can give birth so late.

Another six months passed without sign of a baby. Just looking at her made him tired, she was so thin and worn-out. When she began to complain of nausea and dizziness, sometimes vomiting, sometimes uncontrollably, he was beside himself with worry, but also allowed himself a secret joy.

"Not that," she said sorrowfully. "The Americans sprayed toxic chemicals six times on the forest I lived in. Since then I've been sick like this every once in a while."

A lump swelled in his throat.

Commander Hung visited them frequently, often touting Northern remedies that could "extend youth and prevent old age." He himself drove to Hospital 17 to fetch Lieutenant Colonel Le Giau, his comrade from the war of resistance against the French colonialists and an illustrious obstetrician. A good-natured and soft-hearted person, Doctor Giau heard the couple's story from the division commander and enthusiastically agreed to be their private physician. The doctor prescribed medicines that could only be found in the city to rally her health. Chi took the doctor's prescriptions and letter of recommendation to Da Nang and Hue, searching relentlessly for the medicines, including those most scarce.

Each night, he held her tightly in his arms, and each night, she felt their powerlessness more and more. One night, she placed her hand on his nose to wake him up, then she hugged him and cried. She would not have had the heart to misuse him like that if he would have given her a baby before going to war. A baby! Without a child, the sting of missing him multiplied over the years. During her service in the forest, whenever she heard news that another unit would soon pass through, she waited restlessly, unable to sit still. She waited, then cried each time beside the cookfire. Once, when posted to Station 26, she heard a rumor that he was stopping for a short while at Station 34, so she bundled cooked rice in banana leaves and walked continuously for two days. Once she arrived, she collapsed with exhaustion after learning the man there named Chi was not her husband. This man had a distant wife, too. He held her hands and said, "Go back, and go back happily. You should think that you have met with him. And I will think that I have met with my wife. Sometimes in war we have to delude ourselves to live." She would never forget these words. She returned to Station 26, trying to cling to that delusion of happiness to help her traverse the thirty difficult kilometers, including a section of forest that had been recently sprayed with chemicals. Leaves fell all around her. She ran hastily and fell flat on her face by a spring. When she regained consciousness, the chief of her military station stood over her. "Did you see him?" he asked. Tears flowing, she nodded: "Yes." Eleven years had passed since that day. Maybe because of that toxic demon I cannot have a baby. The idea overwhelmed her suddenly, and she sat up, sweating profusely.

Eventually, she began to notice happiness returning to them. One day, while looking up at his aged face sprayed with sweat, her eyes moistened with tears. She shuddered as a cool sensation washed from her heels to her lips. She pulled him down and kissed him. Surprised only for a moment, he quickly surrendered. She slipped into his arms and smiled.

Happiness really came to her not long after that. But she didn't tell him right away, waiting anxiously instead until she could be sure. A month later, she raised her shirtfront and saw that her nipples had turned a dark purple. She regarded her breasts with great anticipation as they gradually swelled with milk, making her smile contentedly. But before she found the right moment to tell him, she became ill again, vomiting and hot with fever, requiring him to stay home from work to care for her. Exhausted from the pain of her illness, she could also feel her dear baby beginning to take shape. On the third day, after she had regained some of her strength, she leaned against him and whispered:

"I'm pregnant."

He cried with joy, held her tight, and asked, "Is it true? Let me see!"

"See what?" She blushed for shame and shoved at him playfully.

He sat awkwardly beside her and gently shook her by the shoulders. "It's true, isn't it?"

She did not answer him, but quietly kissed his gaunt cheek-bones. That night, he sat up smoking until morning. Even though she told him to come to bed a dozen times, he never slept a wink.

After the military administration's daily meeting that morning, he said to the division commander, "Brother Hung, my wife . . . she's pregnant!"

Commander Hung looked up. "Really? For sure? Did you have an exam?"

He smiled and scratched his head. "I know without an exam. My wife said so . . . for sure. One month and five days already . . ."

Hung twitched his collar. He did so when he was moved. "Good! So good!"

He turned to pass on the "news of the day" to the other officers still milling about from the meeting: "Fresh news: Colonel Chi is going to have a baby!"

Everyone cheered and shook hands, shook hands and laughed, laughed and chatted gaily. He laughed so much his eyes began to tear.

A day later, at the division's residential district, everyone was talking about the fact that Lanh and Colonel Chi were going to have a baby. Officers' wives came to congratulate her. They told her how to take care of the child in the womb, what to eat and what not to, what to know about sleep. She listened to them carefully, but after a while her mind began to drift, imagining her baby: handsome and chubby, toddling unsteadily toward his grandmother, calling to his papa and waving. The noise around her settled, floating on the air like a lullaby.

Late at night, after sleeping for a while, she woke and found him searching for something in his suitcase. She sat up in the bed and looked at him. He glanced back, saying merrily, "Here it is!"

He showed her the picture taken when he was a boy.

"Our son will look like me . . . like this."

She looked at him askance. "We don't know whether it's a son or a daughter."

Stunned, as if the thought had not occurred to him, he cleared his throat and then laughed, "Anyway, it will look like me."

Another month passed, and then another. She began to walk awkwardly. Her skin became more and more pale, even as he tried to bolster her health as much as possible. Commander Hung gave her a liter of bee's honey mixed with rice wine and egg yolk. Doctor Giau rode his bicycle to visit her regularly. While enjoying the happiest period of her life, she became ill again and had to be admitted to the hospital. This time it was so serious that sometimes Commander Hung stayed up all night with Chi in the corridor outside her room. Doctor Giau himself treated her. He found that to make her dream come true had become his own personal aspiration, especially considering the serious nature of her illness. She was not only anemic, as was often the case with women her age, but also she suffered these strange other symptoms. He knew the defoliants' dioxin had permeated her body. All the chemical analyses of her blood pointed to such a conclusion. Of course he tried to conceal it from them. He struggled patiently with her disease, and being confident of his own professional capabilities, he never lost hope.

Each time she recovered from one of the spells of nausea, fever, and fatigue, she left the hospital weaker and paler. As her due date approached, she could barely walk. Chi spent every second by her side, literally becoming her crutch. She grew more and more enervated, but the signs on her face of a pregnant woman's joy did not diminish in the least.

At night, he would fold up her shirt, pressing his ear to her belly to listen to the sound of his baby. He listened seriously and patiently. When he lay down, he could see the goat horn bell hanging from the ceiling. It had been at his side for fourteen years over many battlefields. A comrade had given it to him just before he died, saying, "Whenever you win a battle, ring it to let me be happy." He never forgot that charge. The goat's horn had been polished smooth and intricately carved. Its tinkle sounded like the laughter of children. After victory day, he hung it from the ceiling. When his son—he himself did not know why he always thought it would be a son, and yet he did—when his son grew up, when he was one year old, he would give the bell to him. Keeping the bell his whole life would be his son's duty, so that when his parents came to their final resting place, whenever he had some success, he could ring it to make them happy.

He sat up again, lifted her shirt, and pressed his ear against her belly to listen to the baby.

"That's enough!" she said gently. "You're disturbing our baby."

But he did not agree. "Shh! Let me see if he has any ideas."

She burst out laughing. Suddenly she was curious too. "Does he have any ideas?"

He glanced up, answering objectively, "No. He agrees with us completely. But why do I hear tee-ee, tee-ee—is he bugling?"

She pushed him lightly. "Old man! Go to the devil!"

He laughed. "Soon I will give him the bell, so he won't have to bugle." He hugged her. "I will go and ask for a girl's hand for my son when he is sixteen."

"'My son . . . '"

"I'm sure he's a son. I dreamt he and I were going to his wife's father's house."

The day of the baby's birth finally came.

She trembled entering the labor ward, a nurse on either side holding her hands up the three stairs to the delivery room. Doctor Giau stood waiting at the door. He would deliver her child himself because he knew for sure it would be a difficult case. Just behind her came her husband, Commander Hung, and nearly sixty officers of the division, anxiously looking toward her. Doctor Giau waved his hand, signaling for them all to relax, and closed the door.

One hour . . . two hours . . . three hours . . . Chi drank several glasses of water. Sometimes Commander Hung twitched his collar. A few officers put their ears to the slit of the door and waited for a cry of a baby. Four hours . . . five hours . . . A nurse opened the door and stepped out. Immediately the officers stopped her.

"What's happening?"

"Mrs. Lanh has given birth already," the nurse said with a quavering voice. She smiled. "A son."

"Ah! Hurrah!"

Everyone leapt for joy. Commander Hung hugged Chi and shook him by the shoulders, whirling him about with happiness.

He touched the bell in his pocket, beaming with the anticipation of placing it in his own son's small hand.

In the labor ward, she asked, exhausted, "Boy or girl?" and smiled happily when Doctor Giau said: "You have a son." An old nurse brought the baby to the recovery room and washed him in the endothermic bathtub. Doctor Giau leaned on the medicine chest and breathed heavily, mulling over what he had tried to ignore. The baby was deformed. His left leg folded back, inflexible. His face was distorted frightfully: the left eyelid swelled out, covering the whole cheek-bone. His lower lip swelled too, sloping down toward the chin. No! The Creator is not so merciless. The dioxin, which had accumulated at such high levels in her body, caused these mutations.

The old nurse did her job with a strange imperturbable posture. Suddenly, the doctor hated her. He felt stifled and short of breath. "Water!" he called. "Give me some water."

An assistant from the office hurried in with a glass of water. Passing by the baby, she stopped, transfixed with surprise, and stepped back. The glass fell and shattered. She quickly squatted back on her heels. Then she looked up at Doctor Giau.

He said nothing, sighed a gentle breath, and stepped toward the window. He opened it halfway and looked out. In the yard, dozens of soldiers had gathered around the newborn baby's father. He held the goat horn bell aloft, declaring:

"I will go and ask for a girl's hand for my son when he is sixteen."

The tinkling of the goat horn bell sounded like the laughter of a baby.

Hue, 1985

TRANSLATED BY TRAN THI QUYNH HOA AND CHARLES WAUGH

GRACE

I was researching an essay about Tet for a magazine when my Aunt Thao came to see me. With her eyes swollen and face pale, it seemed like she'd been up all night.

"What's wrong, Auntie? How are Duyen and Mung?"

Aunt Thao covered her face with her hands and wept. "I don't know what to do. You have to help me."

"What is it?" I said impatiently. "My article . . ."

"What article could be as important as helping your aunt?" she snapped. "Oh god! I'll carry this on my face. It's so disgraceful . . ."

Feeling pity for my aunt settle over my heart, I pretended not to know the story. "Have a seat, Auntie," I said. "Tell me everything, and I'll think of a way to help."

Aunt Thao was the youngest daughter of my paternal grandparents, and in her youth the most beautiful woman in her district. My prosperous grandparents spared nothing for her, making sure she enjoyed all the best in her life and education.

At twenty, fortune smiled upon her again: she was the only person in the whole village to receive a scholarship for vocational training in Germany. But it wasn't just luck. She had to take tests and compete against others from all the villages and finally from the district. She'd already earned a high pass on her level-two exams, plus she was the sister of my father, a well-respected commune president. Without my father, what chance did Aunt Thao have to fly to a fairyland like East Germany?

Later, I knew Thao had little happiness living abroad. In the letters she sent me, she explained that my father had insisted she go to Germany because he wanted to separate her from Uncle Toan, who lived in a nearby village. Toan's parents had been landlords. With my father, the commune president, former guerilla fighter against the French, and vice-secretary of the local Party committee, what chance was there he'd give his younger sister in marriage to a guy with a record like that?

I knew many things about Uncle Toan. At my middle school, all the kids my age looked up to him. He earned the best grades in our high school and won several provincial math and literature contests. Besides that, he played great soccer, plus the mandolin and harmonica. The truly sad thing for him was his family's reputation, which proved difficult to escape in such a small village. After high school, he tried to enlist but to no avail. When Thao left for East Germany, Toan spiraled into decline. He refused to come home, instead living in a tent used for raising ducks situated at the edge of a vast, swampy rice field.

Everyone thought the connection between Thao and Toan would be broken, since they'd each gone in a different direction. Meanwhile, the war went on fiercely, and Toan tried to enlist again. This time, the village committee could not refuse him. A month later, he marched into South Vietnam.

After four years, Aunt Thao finally returned from East Germany. She had a radiant beauty and, given the current living conditions, was considered quite wealthy. She brought back several boxes of foreign goods for her family, including fur coats, Diamond brand bicycles, watches, and wool thread. By that time, I had begun my studies at the university, and I couldn't have been happier to get a bright blue Diamond bike as a gift. But like they say, *Money spread is soon gone*, and Aunt Thao went to work in a factory, living in the dormitory like everyone else. Despite her brilliant, abundant beauty, she continued to be lonely. Over the years, many men called on her, trying to win her favor. She rejected them all. She seemed completely indifferent to the calls of youth and love. I wondered at the time if her indulgent life in Germany had made it so she'd never be happy here again.

But I had misunderstood. The love between Thao and Toan still burned hot and bright. Both had kept a promise to wait for each other. In 1974, when Uncle Toan had been wounded in battle and taken to a hospital in Ninh Binh, Thao went to see him immediately. That's when they made plans to be married. By this time, it was ten years they'd spent apart, but even though they were no longer young, their affection was as fresh and fervent as ever. At the wedding, my father—the former commune president—came to Ninh Binh himself to preside over the ceremony and bring the couple together. He wept for the years of theirs he'd wasted.

Finally it seemed Uncle Toan and Aunt Thao had become happy people.

After ten years of fighting, Uncle Toan could at last hang up the overcoat of his bad reputation. He had received a medal for valor, became an officer, and began to rise through the ranks. Back in the North, the army sent him to the military academy, and after that they stationed him in Hanoi. Meanwhile Aunt Thao proved herself at the factory, becoming its assistant manager. She requested a house from the property distribution system, and later it became one of the most valuable properties in the city.

Over the next two years, Aunt Thao gave birth to a son first, Mung, and then a daughter, Duyen. With this formula for child-birth, people said their family must have great luck. The names themselves, Mung (Happiness) and Duyen (Grace), expressed all that Thao and Toan wanted from life. When their children grew up and began school, our whole family regarded them as little angels. Mung was healthy, handsome, and intelligent. And Duyen was very beautiful. Everyone kept saying she would grow up to be Miss Vietnam.

And so, of course, disaster struck.

When Mung turned eight, his hair fell out and his legs began to weaken. By the time he was ten, he could no longer walk. Then it was Duyen's turn. She also lost her hair, and tumors began to form all over her body. Her eyes bulged out, and her memory deteriorated. In no time, Uncle Toan and Aunt Thao spent nearly every cent they had on treatment. Hearing of an intelligent doctor or a well-known herbalist, they rushed to find him. But nothing worked. The doctors all concluded the same thing: Mung and Duyen had begun to manifest signs of genetic mutation from dioxin, the result of Toan's repeated exposure to toxic defoliants during his ten years in the jungle.

Now the children were no longer a source of pride and happiness but a miserable and heavy burden. Mung lay in the corner of the room all day, eating, drinking, and relieving himself on the floor. Duyen appeared crazy, sometimes grinning, sometimes sobbing, all without apparent cause. My Uncle Toan and Aunt Thao aged rapidly, always being so sad and haggard. Fortunately, because the back of their house opened to the main street, they were able to switch the front door for the back and open a small grocery store. This way they could be at home and still earn a living.

The years flew by, and Duyen had turned eighteen already. Her thin hair made her look like a typhoid survivor, and her stunted body had grown no bigger than a thirteen-year-old child's, but she was still a young woman, with curves in her hips and breasts and a curiosity about love and sex. The tragedy for Duyen and for my aunt and uncle was in this very point. Duyen was like a bomb that failed to explode, and since everyone assumed it never would explode, no one ever made an effort to defuse it.

But then, of course, the bomb did explode. With all the love and worry of a mother, Aunt Thao discovered Duyen had gotten pregnant. God almighty, it was truly terrible. It would've been bad enough for a healthy girl, but with Duyen?

Aunt Thao questioned her. At first, she just kept laughing foolishly, denying everything. Aunt Thao had to draw her in, to bribe her. She promised a big wedding, and to let the couple run the store on the first floor. Duyen listened to her mother and, seduced by her imagination, told the whole story of how she and the boy treated one another and how they made love.

It could have been worse. The guy who slept with her was San, the son of one of Uncle Toan's comrades. He had graduated from high school but for three years in a row failed to pass the university's entrance exam. Uncle Toan helped him get a job as watchman at a joint-venture company earning two hundred bucks a month. He was tall and chubby, but handsome, and he could also be sneaky and often spoke without thinking. Because of his parents' close friendship with Thao and Toan, he came to their house most weekends and lived there as freely as at his own home. As they say, *Even wet straw near a fire will eventually burn.* As Duyen's body filled out, she looked attractive and alluring. But San foolishly didn't expect the fun he had with her to produce such serious consequences. When the secret came out, he did what all irresponsible boys do: he disappeared without a trace, thinking only one thing: "Escape!"

"What a mess," I said to my aunt. "You can't make them get married, and San obviously isn't interested; he only used her for fun."

"It's because it's such a mess that only you can save us." Aunt Thao locked her nervous eyes on mine, imploring me to help her. "You have to convince San and his family to make some kind of agreement to let us take him as a husband for Duyen. We'll give them whatever dowry they want."

"Why hatch such a crazy plan?" I said, irritated by her dragging me into it. "An abortion makes more sense. It's certainly more expedient. Besides, there's no way Duyen can actually be a real mother."

She began to sob again. "Try to understand our situation," she sniffed. "It's like Mung has already left us. We will have to take care of Duyen for the rest of our lives. But as bleak as the situation is, maybe there's also just a tiny bit of hope. Maybe she'll give birth to a healthy son, a boy who'll bring us joy and take care of us when we're old. Your uncle and I discussed it, and we both think it's the best way. If San leaves her a week or two after the wedding, who cares?"

"Oh, Auntie," I sighed, choking back my tears. "I'll do what I can. I'll go to San and his parents. I'll get them to make a deal."

Just as I expected, San denied everything flat out. His impudent face appeared indifferent as I told him about Duyen's pregnancy. But I am not a moderate person. I know how to work a kid like that. "I don't think you want us to make this public by forcing you to have a blood test," I said. "Duyen told us everything. You can either accept the generous proposal from Duyen's family and continue to live in a good house in Hanoi with an income of two hundred dollars per month, or you can be fired from the company and return to the countryside to work with the buffalo."

Naturally, San couldn't take much of this kind of talk. After a while, he confessed everything.

"So, we'll plan a wedding for the day before Tet," I said.

"God no!" he exclaimed. "Don't make me marry Duyen. Take pity. I'll pay to take her to the hospital."

"Abort the baby so you can run away? I don't think so." I continued to badger him: "Everyone here will know you got her pregnant. As a colonel, her father won't suffer a disgrace caused by your bad behavior. He was on his way to speak with the director of your company yesterday, until I intervened."

San froze, his face pale and desperate.

I clapped him on the shoulder and said, "Don't worry. I calmed my uncle down. And don't be afraid to get married. No one wants you to be bound by this. After the wedding, say a week or so, you can slip away. My aunt and uncle just want to pretend to have a wedding for Duyen to save face with the neighbors. Don't you get it?"

He was too slow. He looked at me suspiciously.

"Listen. Man-to-man, I'm telling you like it is. Not doing this would be stupid."

Tears came to San's eyes. He said, "Okay. I have no choice."

"Good," I said. "Now the second step: tomorrow we'll go to your home village to talk to your parents about the wedding."

"Are you kidding?" San took my hand, begging me. "It would kill me if people in my village and my parents find out about this. I'll make the arrangements for the wedding by myself. Can't you let me do that?"

He was so shameful, so afraid of ridicule. Still, I thought, he is handsome. Maybe I shouldn't force him to marry a girl not suitable for him. Finding some sympathy for him, as disgraceful as he was, I didn't want to drag this out. Suddenly I had the answer: I would find some people to act as his relatives. It would be a very strange wedding with only one real family member on the groom's side, but on the other hand, with the new market economy, play-acting was all there was. The unemployed always gathered at the street corners, so it took just one shout to put together thirty people to act as the "groom's house."

In all my life, I'd never seen a wedding like this, much less directed one. Uncle Toan and Aunt Thao looked worn out. Despite their sadness, they pretended to be happy, but couldn't quite manage to really smile properly. For his part, I must say San acted the role of groom very well. He kept his mouth shut and put on a solemn face, looking like he'd just became a young and happy husband but without forgetting that he was shouldering the responsibility for a new family.

The groom's "family" were obviously the most happy. They talked and laughed like firecrackers going off, eating and drinking as much as possible. They stuffed themselves even more greedily than the characters in the Nguyen Cong Hoan story "A Feast." And not only did they eat like pigs, but they stuffed their pockets too, cramming them full of candy, cookies, and Vina cigarettes. It was a shame, but what else could be done?

Duyen played the most distinguished role in the whole wedding party. I barely recognized her. Her white wedding dress and professionally styled wig reduced her ugliness quite a lot, though her overdone makeup and dazzling white teeth made her look a little like a wooden puppet.

There were no firecrackers, but the peach trees in the garden had bloomed, signaling that spring and the new year had come. But the blossoms didn't remind me of the coming year. Instead, when the wind blew, scattering the petals to the ground, it unexpectedly reminded me of the defoliated jungles where my Uncle Toan lived for nearly ten years. More than twenty years have passed since then, but it still haunts us. It might even keep haunting us if it continues to grow from seeds like the one in Duyen's belly.

My cousin took my hand and laughed with her wide open mouth. She said, "Hoang, take a picture of San and me under the peach tree."

I looked at her and my heart lurched. Poor girl. What would be next for her?

I wished her good luck. Named as she was, I hoped the spring might also bring her a little grace.

Hanoi, 1995

TRANSLATED BY CHARLES WAUGH AND HUY LIEN

A DREAM

One year after the Liberation of the South, Cuong finally returned to his village from military service. A year was a long time for his family to wait, even for everyone in the village, but what they did not know was that Cuong had spent that year in a military hospital. On the very last day of the war, as Cuong and his unit marched to Saigon from the southwest under the command of the 232 Front, a wicked piece of shrapnel severed his right arm. But, in war, such a wound does not cause a big fuss. And Cuong's late return was absolutely ordinary. Extremely ordinary!

After a while, Cuong's life also became ordinary. The red badge awarded to a wounded soldier and his empty sleeve turned him from a run-of-the-mill peasant into a town hero, a recognizable soldier whom they made the guard of the newly built City House of Compassion. This turn of fate suited Cuong well, putting him at ease with his past and present and, of course, with his future also. For him, nothing could prevent him from having a splendid future. No one could or had a right to doubt this fact.

Soon after starting this new life, Cuong got married. His wife, Hoàn, taught at a district school. She had been Cuong's special friend since they were little children. Together, they shared many childhood memories, as well as the great longing they felt for each other during the months they'd spent apart. His wedding was not special. It was as ordinary as other postwar weddings. One month, then two months passed, then plenty of signals helped them realize something new. Words could not express Cuong's happiness. Every night, touching Cuong's cut-off arm, Hoàn murmured lovely things as she fell into sleep. Meanwhile, Cuong stroked his hand over his wife's soft, smooth belly and felt the warmth spreading.

One night, Cuong asked, "Boy or girl?"

"I don't know," replied his wife. "If it is a boy, we'll call him Cường, right? Cuong and Cường, that's nice!"

"Yeah! And if it's a girl, call her Hoan? Lien Hoan. That's good!"

"You just like to party! What a monkey!"

"A monkey . . . ?"

Then they slept, holding each other tightly.

When she went into labor, Cuong brought his wife to the hospital. Anxiously, he waited outside the labor ward. Everything went quickly. Right after his wife's labor groans stopped, a short cry rang out, "Waa-waa-waa."

Cuong froze.

From the labor ward, the doctor's voice came to him like from another world: "A girl . . . you have a girl."

A daughter! From that moment, Cuong became someone else. A real father!

Two years later, Cuong and his wife were still in shock. Destiny? No, it was not destiny. Both explicably and inexplicably, the mere existence of this child alone engendered sorrow. The baby had an ordinary face, but half her body defied belief. No one can imagine such a merciless Creator! A large hump on her back seemed to be trying to fold her body in half. Despite the abnormally mottled flesh of her arms and legs, her face was very pretty. Heartbreakingly pretty!

She had shining black hair, light skin, limpid eyes, and rose-red lips. Especially exceptional, her fresh smile looked as pure and arrogant as if the girl were flouting the powerlessness of human beings to the Creator. As with other cases, the doctors diagnosed the baby's illness as exposure to dioxin, the toxic chemical her father absorbed during the war. Despite her condition, the baby's parents named her as they had decided before her birth, Hoan.

More than two years old, Hoan could not do anything but smile. She always had a smile on her lips. The older she grew, the more arrogant it became. After the cry at birth, no sound at all had emerged from her well-shaped mouth. She lived totally without sound, and so did her parents. Cuong and his wife seemed to not want to interrupt the silent life of their daughter. Without discussing it, they each developed the habit of communicating nonverbally. Together, each night, Hoàn and Cuong tucked the sheet below the poor baby's chin. As time passed, their love for their daughter increased, but Cuong and his wife wanted a real daughter more than anything else. But the dioxin in Cuong's blood frustrated them sorrowfully. How could they fight against destiny?

And then one day, fate suddenly shook them out of their silent life. Hoan was five years old, but her body had grown very little. The year before, Cuong had moved to a home next to the City House of Compassion, and Hoàn had become a teacher to the orphaned children living there. Their sorrow had not been eased, but at least their life had become stable and peaceful. Their pains, caused by Cuong's missing arm and their daughter's abnormal body, had to some extent been soothed by Hoàn's incredible love for her small family. That day, just as dawn began to glow upon the town walls, Cuong had already begun his walk to work next door, for some reason anxious enough to have left half an hour early. A premonition urged haste for something that seemed really important. As Cuong approached the building's front gate, the weak cry of a baby stopped him suddenly. It lay beneath a jackfruit tree, wrapped tightly in a bundle of clothes. He practically yanked the bundle from the ground and quickly unwrapped the gasping, nearly unconscious baby. Someone must have laid it there just a few moments before. Cuong felt a heat spread over his body as his heartbeat pounded. Clutching the baby, he raced home. When Cuong's wife took the baby from him, little Hoan surprisingly broke her silence, sputtering out some unintelligible words, stunning her parents. They knew the baby's appearance had to be fate.

All went well. The baby girl was just one day old, according to a short letter found in the swaddling clothes. An unfortunate woman must have had to leave her daughter to the House of Compassion. And perhaps she had left her just before Cuong arrived. Given their situation, Cuong and his wife had no trouble fulfilling the requirements for adoption. They named her Cường—the name planned for Hoan had she been a boy.

Time flew by quickly. Cường grew up to be a very pretty girl. Her sister, Hoan, still seemed like a little kid but with an adult's face. Hoan had been able to babble ever since Cường had joined their family. Even though her words could not be understood, they warmed her parents' hearts. Cuong and his wife nearly forgot the time of their misfortune years ago. Hoan and Cường became strongly attached to one another. Cường loved her sister. Except for going to school and doing housework, Cường spent all day long with her. They clung together like grains of cooked rice. Watching his daughters play together, Cuong could not help crying tears of joy.

One day when Cường was eight, a white car stopped in front of the house. Cường was at school, and Hoàn was teaching, while Cuong looked after Hoan at home. Just one glance at the woman who emerged made Cuong's heart writhe with pain. She and Cường looked exactly alike. She didn't pull out her hair, beg Cuong, or otherwise make a scene. She came only to ask for forgiveness. In this way, Cường's mother came back after many difficult years.

By visiting frequently, and through Cuong and Hoàn's kind-hearted help, the woman soon became close to Cường. But little Hoan began to behave erratically, sometimes crying, at others laughing hysterically. After many days of heart-breaking consideration, Cuong and Hoàn made the decision to allow Cường to live with her real mother. Not because the woman had realized her mistake or had become rich enough to care for her, but because they knew how significant a daughter was in life.

The unfortunate woman seemed surprised to receive such extreme happiness. No one told Cường the reason her birth mother had abandoned her. Of course, Cường did not want to be far from her parents and sister. Nevertheless, on a beautiful day, she left with the lady in the white car. Hoan watched her little sister go. Then she cried and cried and cried.

When she finally stopped crying, Hoan also stopped eating, babbling, and laughing. By the fourth day of silence, Cuong and Hoàn became panic-stricken, totally powerless to remedy their daughter's situation. Soon, Hoan no longer responded to her father's touch. She stopped breathing, even though her face remained beautiful, as pure as an angel's. Cuong's wife collapsed. As if walking in his sleep, Cuong clutched at his wife and daughter. With his one remaining hand, he could not embrace them both.

Cuong looked impotently at his empty sleeve. He did not yet understand his life up to that moment had been just like a beautiful dream.

Hanoi, 1974

TRANSLATED BY TRAN THI QUYNH HOA AND CHARLES WAUGH

HOANG MINH TUONG

THE STORY OF A FAMILY

The staff at the hospital all said Khang was a man deeply in love with his wife. Everyone was impressed with how he cared for Tra during her long, six-month recovery, and the female medical students in particular enjoyed telling the couple's romantic love story. He was a young man from Da Nang who had moved to the North in '66 and had studied in the Soviet Union. She was a famous fighter in Saigon who began working undercover at the age of twelve. Late in the war, the Saigon government imprisoned her in Da Lat until the day of liberation. They met and fell in love with each other as sudden as summer thunder in 1979. He was attracted to her graceful face, supple body, and especially her well-known feat of arms. And she'd fallen in love with him before they'd even met, just by hearing what people said about him. He fit the idea of her perfect man: a brilliant face, big and gentle eyes, a mixture of southern and northern accent in his voice, and a deep intellect from his training abroad.

Hearing the staff all talking about them, I looked for a chance to get acquainted.

But I was puzzled when I first saw Tra. By then, she didn't look like a famous fighter from Saigon. She was so small, thin, and pale that she looked like a twelve- or thirteen-year-old girl. Her body took up just a tiny bit of the center of the bed. Her dark blue veins pulsed visibly beneath the transparent skin of her bone-thin arms.

"How is she?" I asked Khang hesitantly.

He looked at me with his sad eyes and must have been moved by my sympathetic expression. He bent toward Tra and removed the scarf covering her head.

Her appearance was startling. Her polished and shiny scalp had no hair, making her shriveled face look like a skull.

"The doctors say she's sick with a disease caused by the war," said Khang. "We're waiting for the final test results. They think she's got dioxin poisoning from her prison being so close to one of the Americans' chemical stockpiles. The doctors removed her ovaries last month. A tumor is now growing in her breast."

I wiped the sweat from my face and asked Khang sympathetically, "Do you have any children?"

He shook his head once and breathed a sigh.

After that day, Khang and I became good friends. I'd visit Tra in her room at the hospital, then walk with Khang beneath the shade trees in the hospital's garden.

One day, he said, "You know, both Tra and I happened to have important things happen at twelve, even though I'm six years older. That's when Tra left Da Nang with her family and moved to Saigon, where she began to spy for the NLF. At the same age, I also left Da Nang, but instead I went north, walking along the Ho Chi Minh Trail."

"You walked the Ho Chi Minh Trail at twelve?"

He took my being impressed as ignorance of the many unusual achievements teenagers accomplished during the war. "Now in peaceful times, my family's story always seems unbelievable. But then, the fate of each of my family members was also the fate of thousands of other people. My father left for the North in 1954, just before I was born. During my childhood, I had no father. Every time I asked my mother about him, she pointed at the mountains in the west and said: 'Your father is over there.' What was 'over there' was the Quang Nam—Da Nang resistance base at the spur of the Ho Chi Minh Trail that passed through my motherland, Go Noi.

"In 1966, I joined a team of dozens of kids who volunteered to go north for training. At the same time, my father had received orders to head south to establish a guerrilla base, and just by chance, we met one another for the first time at a communication station on the Ho Chi Minh Trail. Tall and handsome, he had a ruddy face and bright, black eyes. Later I knew he had just graduated from a military school in the Soviet Union and had volunteered for this mission. Before leaving Hanoi for the South, he had learned of my trip to the North and arranged to meet me.

"'Hey Khang! It's me, your father,' he said as he bent forward and pressed his warm cheek to mine. 'Of course you don't recognize me.' Our tears mingled and I pressed my face close to his chest.

"We had only half an hour together in the forest along the trail. He had to set off with his unit and I had to hurry to catch up with my team. But before leaving, he put seventy dong in my hand, the whole of his one-month salary that he'd saved while in the North.

"I didn't know it would be the only time we met. He returned to Go Noi later that year to organize the resistance to the Saigon regime. He died not long after that near our ancestral lands. I only learned about it afterward, while studying in the Soviet Union."

"So you had no contact with your family for a long, long time," I said.

"Absolutely none! I lived with my friends at school in Hanoi and at the university. My family all those years were the command in the North and my friends. I felt lonely a lot, especially around Tet. But I always tried to get news about my parents. When I graduated from the Soviet university in 1978 and could finally come home, I immediately went straight to Go Noi, not even bothering to go through all the paperwork at the Ministry of Education. You've heard about Go Noi, right?"

"Of course. Everyone's heard the stories about how fierce the fights were there."

"That's right, that's my homeland. Site of the bloodiest conflicts in Quang Da district during the war. It used to be famous for its mulberry trees and silkworm breeding. By the time I got home, it had been completely laid bare, devastated. My grandmother, aunt, and mother were all still alive. They were the greatest women I've ever known. If we ever have a chance to meet in Da Nang, I'll take you to Go Noi."

A year later, I arranged a trip with Khang to his homeland. It's where the Thu Bon river joins the Vu Gia, about thirty kilometers from Da Nang. The river is deep blue there, and the red earth dotted with many fragrant lotus ponds. I've heard Go Noi was even more beautiful before the war. The mulberry fields stretched as far as the eye could see, and the flat land nearest the river resounded with the clacking of the looms. A famous image of the area depicted the silhouettes of slender women carrying baskets of silkworms. Because of their smooth, white complexion and graceful bodies, people regarded these Go Noi women as the most beautiful in Dien Ban district.

Khang's more than eighty-year-old grandmother lived with her daughter, Tram, who was in her fifties, in a house built by the local commune. Tram was a former guerilla who spent her whole youth fighting the American and South Korean troops in hundreds of battles. She fought so much, she never made time for marriage, which is why she ended up spending her golden years with her mother.

At noon I sat in the living room while these two women told me about what had happened in their lives. Seeing the three certificates of martyrdom for Khang's grandfather, father, and uncle on the wall, I gave my attention to these two with great appreciation. Khang was right: "They are the greatest women." And there was still another one like them in this family I had not yet met!

After spending the day with them, we were sad to have to say good-bye. On the way home, Khang surprised me with news from his grandmother about his brother, Dung.

"I didn't even know you had a brother!" I said.

"Not just one, but two. Grandma said Dung's application for the Orderly Departure Program has just been approved."

"Really? That's strange, I thought the O.D. program was only for former Saigon government officers and their families, sponsored by the Americans."

"That's right. Dung's not my father's son. My mother had him six years after me, in 1960. That year was the worst one in the South. My father had gone north in '54, leaving his pregnant wife only because he thought the South would follow the Geneva agreement and he'd be back in two years. But that didn't happen, and he couldn't see his wife for many years. Now I understand his love for her was what made him one of the first volunteers to return South. As soon as he arrived in Go Noi, he sent a message to my mother instructing her to meet him in the forest near the base. I'm sure she was excited to see him, but at the same time, she must've had a great fear deep in her heart. After six years of separation, of course it was wonderful for them to see each other, but do you know what happened in that little forest shack?"

I shook my head, not wanting to interrupt.

"My father nearly killed her." Khang couldn't stop himself from breathing a sigh. "Right at the moment they first embraced, he knew she was pregnant."

Just imagining the scene in that shack made me shiver: in the dim light of the cabin, he pulled near to him the body that had given him so much happiness and longing, a body that trembled with fear and shame. Her heart must have skipped a beat when his big, strong hand caressed her belly.

"Oh my god," he gasped. "You're pregnant? With who? Say it, with who! Why would you come to me carrying this terrible thing inside?"

Though whispered, his words broke like a thunderclap. His hands went cold, as if cut from his arms. He pulled the κ54 pistol from its holster. "I'll kill you."

"Do it," she replied. "I am the utter disgrace of our family. I don't have the heart to live any more. Only death can release me."

The gun slipped from his hand, clattering on the ground. He shook her, asking, "What happened? Who did this? Tell me, I'll kill him."

"I'm guilty," she sobbed. "I wasn't strong enough to be faithful. I beg you, kill me, please, you couldn't kill all of them. These past six years, the South has become a prison. No woman whose husband went north can live without fear."

He sat as if turned to stone, the anger, compassion, and sadness all roiling together inside him.

Khang shook his head. "That night was the most tragic event in my father's life. After it, his heart bled for the misfortune of his family. In his mind, he knew my mother could not be blamed; it was the Southern regime and their anti-Communist Law 10–59 and the guillotines they carried everywhere throughout the South that had made life difficult for the women whose husbands had gone north. But he could only forgive my mother years later, the next time he returned home. Dung, my half brother, was about five or six. Even if he wasn't from my father's line, my grandma and aunt treated him as such and loved him dearly. Before I went north, I thought he was my real brother, my father's son. But now he's about to leave for the U.S. He's very close to my mother. He loves her very much. It's him, not me, who's supported her all these years."

"Do you know his real father?"

"He left Saigon for the U.S one day before the liberation army took the city. I've seen the letter and picture he sent from Florida. He was an officer in the Saigon Army, stationed in the '60s in Da Nang."

"How do you feel about him going to America?"

"I have no idea. It's up to him to decide. If he goes, he could be a lot of help to my mother when she grows old. But even so, I hope he stays."

The next time I saw Khang, he had arranged to bring me to his mother's house.

Hong was sixty, but still held the beauty and elegance of her youth. Her house, four large and well-aired rooms, sat back a little way from Highway 1 in a yard that stretched all the way down to the river.

When we arrived, she had just returned from the market with her groceries balanced on a shoulder pole.

After settling in and saying hello, Hong told me about the house. "I have given it to Dung and his wife. I bought it four years ago, and also another in Da Nang that Khang and his wife live in. Of course, they didn't have enough to buy them. My youngest son, Trung, isn't married and lives in the commune, but I already have a plan to buy him a house when he takes a wife."

"How have you managed to be so clever?"

"I'm not so clever. I earned it all by hand." Hong held up her hands to show me the roughened skin. "When my husband left for the

North, I was pregnant with Khang. I had to feed my mother-in-law and myself, fight the war, and face many other challenges. When they burned our mulberry fields and broke the looms and drove all the villagers to Da Nang, I opened a business at the market. That's how I earned money to feed my family. I even supported my husband, his troops, and a guerilla team. I bought gold too, but in '68, the Americans dropped a bomb in our backyard and blew my little hoard to smithereens."

That afternoon, she told me about meeting her husband when he came home from the North for good. It was 1967, the year after Khang had gone north himself:

"One night, I had just curled up with Dung in my arms and dozed off on the bed when I heard a noise at the door and saw someone cross the moonlight into the room. Frightened, I stood up on the bed with Dung in my arms. 'Who are you?' I cried. The man fastened the door and motioned me to be silent. My goodness! It was Thanh, Khang's father. I'd received a message that he would come to the base soon, but still, his coming in like that was a shock. I wanted so desperately to see him, but I worried he hadn't forgiven me and would not accept Dung. Trembling with fear, I told Dung: 'Your father has come home. That's Khang's father, and yours.' Dung climbed from my arms, took a step forward and nearly hugged Thanh around his legs, but suddenly he stopped and stepped back. 'Father!' he said. 'Where is Khang now?' It surprised me, hearing him call Thanh, a stranger to him, 'Father.' Thanh stood transfixed with amazement. All at once, he stooped down and swept Dung into his arms. 'My son!' he cried, 'I am your father.' I saw two tears glittering on his cheek. His sweet voice told me he forgave me for everything. I rushed to him, tumbling into his chest. All my worry melted into the utmost happiness."

What a strange and wonderful couple! After six years of doubt and longing, they cast aside all suspicion and once again came to live together as happily as in their first days of marriage. These days turned out to be the most time they had together, and the happiest. They lived in a house along the river only occasionally attacked by bursts of gunfire from the Da Nang military base or from American helicopters. But this happiness lasted just a short time. Thanh was killed while Hong was pregnant with Trung, their youngest son. And again, this lovely woman of Go Noi had to raise a son by herself.

Before I had to return to Hanoi, Khang and Tra wanted me to spend the day with them at My Khe beach and then come to a special dinner with their family.

From what I remembered of Tra at the hospital in Hanoi a year ago, I would never have recognized her now. It was like she had become an entirely different woman, with her hair grown back, smooth and shining black and cut short around the sides of her gentle, round face. The joy in her large, clear eyes seemed to say she'd never been sick at all. Tra thanked me for visiting her so often while she'd been in the hospital. Knowing that my girlfriend, Binh, from Hanoi had come with me to Da Nang for business, she invited me to bring her to our picnic at the beach.

At My Khe beach, summer afternoons are lovely. Bicycles and motorbikes pass on the street behind, while people stroll happily along in brightly colored clothing. I had hoped to have the chance to bring my girlfriend here, to see her strut her stuff in her new swimsuit. Not wanting to be the only girl swimming, she asked Tra if she was coming along.

Tra shook her head and said, "You three go ahead and enjoy yourselves. I'll stay here and keep an eye on the bags."

"Oh, come on!" said Binh. "We should all swim together. You can show off your beauty on the beach!"

Tra would not change her mind. Khang whispered to me: "Tra doesn't want to swim. Last year they removed one of her breasts and her ovaries at the hospital in Hanoi, both major operations. Fortunately, the tumors were benign."

During the years Tra had been tortured in the Da Lat prison, she had also suffered from many illnesses. It was no wonder her health was so poor now.

After Binh and I swam, we all tried to make the best of our trip to the beach, but everyone's mood had turned a little somber.

When we returned to Khang's house, we found two more motor-bikes in the middle of the yard, and two men sitting nearby talking and smoking. Right away, I recognized Khang's brother, Trung, who looked every bit like Khang, only younger. Dung took a little more effort. There were some similarities, but also differences—darker skin, a narrower face, more slanted eyes.

I assumed the big party that night would be a going away party for Dung and his wife before they left for the U.S.

When the whole family had gathered later that evening, I kept expecting Khang, as the eldest brother, to give an opening speech, but he had become so withdrawn that he simply stood there holding his cup of Han River beer in his hand, watching everyone else.

"Let's get the party started, Ma," Dung said finally. "Tell us why you invited us all here."

"Yes, let's get started," said Hong. She looked at Khang, then turned her eyes on me. "Today as Mr. Hoang and his girlfriend have come here from the North, we would like to welcome them to this gathering of our big family. Now that we're all here having fun, Dung and Phuong would like to share a few words."

I wondered whether Dung would announce his departure. Khang looked like he was carrying a heavy burden, and his eyes had red-dened as if he might break into tears.

"Ma, you're the head of our family. Please give your speech first."

"Okay, I'll tell you something," said Hong. "Today is Viet's first birthday. Dung and Phuong have discussed the idea carefully and have decided to ask Khang and Tra to adopt him as their own, real son. Because of the war, Tra could not have children. There's no blame there. But as a mother loves a child, I love Khang. I only wish they had a child to live with them and give them happiness, as Khang gave me. We will all see Viet raised as their own son. Dung's wife will certainly have another child."

Khang still did not look happy. He said to Dung, "You two have decided to leave Viet here so you can go?"

"Go where?" asked Hong. After realizing what Khang meant, she turned her eyes to him with a smile. "They aren't going anywhere. Mr. Hoang, you probably know Dung's application to go to America has been approved. But they have decided to stay here, and I agree with them. I gave birth to Dung in Go Noi and he will live in Go Noi forever. His grandmother, his aunt, and I are here now. His father and many people who fought for our country died on this land. We didn't fight the Americans all those years just to have him go live there now. Even if he became happy and successful in the U.S., he would still lose his original identity. I have only three sons, but if any one of them abandoned me, I would have to disown him."

She spoke in a voice choked with emotion. As though a wave crested her cheeks, the tears began to pour from her eyes.

"Goodness, Ma!" exclaimed Dung. "Why cry now?"

Hong wiped away the tears and smiled. "Don't worry, I am laughing now. Let's drink a toast."

Trung raised his glass and said, "Cheers to Ma, whose grandson is one year old today. Cheers to Khang and Tra and Dung and Phuong for this beautiful boy. Cheers to Mr. Hoang and Ms. Binh!"

The clinking of glasses and shouts of congratulations cheered up the room.

I raised my glass to Hong and said: "A toast to your health and happiness, and in thanks for sharing the joy of your family with us today."

I drank my glass of beer to calm my heart, which was overflowing with admiration for this brave old lady. My sight wavered taking in the joyful scene. I wondered, was it the very strong Han River beer, or tears of exaltation?

Da Nang, 1991 – Do Son, 1992
TRANSLATED BY HUY LIEN AND CHARLES WAUGH

MA VAN KHANG

THAY PHUNG

Shabby and strange in strength and appearance, more than anything else Thay* Phung looked like a hollow peanut shell. His small frame measured less than five feet and under ninety pounds. Worse still, he often wore a broad-brimmed conical hat pulled down low on his overly large head, and his short legs splayed like a Chinese eight:

On his feet he wore rough shoes with big toe caps, making him appear even smaller and more freakish.

Kop, kop, kop . . . Thay Phung plodded down the corridor of my province's primary teacher's training college. Certainly he wanted a kind of stateliness. But unfortunately, when he stood, he appeared as dull as a drooping tree, and when he walked, he looked even worse, with his head thrust forward and his arms held back, hurried and miserable.

His secret countenance only appeared when he stood on the dais of a lecture hall in front of his students. "I am Phung," he would say. "*Phung* in Vietnamese means 'swollen' and 'large.' But in Chinese it means 'to meet.' But I am Vu Bat Phung, which means 'to not meet.' To not meet what? To not meet the right time. It means to not keep up with the times. It means . . . when our country has

---

*The word *thay* means "teacher" and is the common form of address for a male teacher, similar to the title *professor* in English but without indicating rank. It is pronounced *tay*, rhyming with *day*.

been invaded, even my volunteering to go to battle is not welcome!"

At these times, he was perfectly suited to his environment. Completely different! He seemed like another Phung, not the stunted and mediocre one, when he stepped out of his everyday façade and showed this side of himself. His face became round and sweet, his cheeks dark pink, his lips like a young unmarried girl's, and his teeth appeared small and even like the seeds of a gourd. Best of all, his voice grew warm and resounding, even noble and charming. At these times he seemed a modern-day mandarin, not only wise and sincere but also capable and amusing. His personality was at the same time high-minded and down-to-earth.

Though he mocked himself, in fact, he was not the one who could not keep up with the times! Toward the end of the American War, when he was nineteen, he volunteered to join the North Vietnamese Army right after graduating from the provincial primary teacher's training college. And finally he was accepted, which meant finally his deceptions succeeded: he drank gallons of water and stuffed himself with food to gain weight; he even stood on tiptoe to be tall enough when they measured. The examiners knew he had cheated, but for his enthusiasm they passed him anyway. Regardless, even though they let him enlist, the army did not treat him like an ordinary recruit. He was not allowed to be in the artillery, the commandos, the engineer corps, or even the infantry. Based on his strength and appearance, they assigned him to guard an isolated munitions depot. And so he spent the entire last five years of the war as just a first-class private guarding a mortar stockpile in a jungle near the Cambodian border. In those five years, the depot was forgotten, and so, of course, was he. But also in those five years, regardless of being forgotten, he continued to do his job. He continued on as an individual, mapping out his own path and following it, regardless of being by himself. In those five years of being alone, he kept the depot safe; not a single shell among thousands was misplaced. In those five years, he planted corn and squash to feed himself and took care of himself when he fell sick. In those five years, spent without a single other person to speak to, he lived in fear of forgetting himself as a human being, of forgetting who he was. Thus, to remind himself of his humanity, he had to work, to think, to meditate, and to move his mouth and his tongue—to talk—continually. But just talking to himself constantly would be boring and nonsensical. So he sang. To himself. All the time. He sang when he tidied up the depot. He sang when he cleaned each of the mortars. He sang when he cleared trees for planting crops. He sang when fixing his tent or building props, henhouses and birdcages. He sang every day and thus found out he had such a warm baritone voice that even all the parrots and hill mynas he raised would seem to forget their own voices just to listen to him.

He sang in loneliness in the middle of the deep jungle. He sang all types of music, from the love duets of Bac Ninh, Co La, or Trong Quan folk songs to modern songs such as "Eden," "Dreamy Stream," or "Moving toward Saigon, Moving toward the Capital." He especially loved to sing the "Song of the Mountain Girl":

Oh Mountain girl! My life is like a bird soaring quickly through
    the sky of time.
Oh Mountain girl! Don't doubt my heart is true now that my
    tears have stopped falling.

He sang without thinking, but in his deep and sad voice the songs also revealed his arrogance and apprehension about the future.

So that was it. Most people went to war with their comrades-at-arms. But he had only himself. Thay Phung sang because he had to manage to survive on his own, depend on himself, and rely on his own handiness. Circumstance was a very good teacher. It developed his natural talents and turned him into a jack-of-all-trades who could do any kind of handiwork better than most people.

Finally the army remembered the forgotten warehouse in the jungle. And only after receiving the whole store of untouched mortar shells did they take him to the hospital.

"You have a tumor in your left lung, comrade!" said the X-ray doctor.

"Really?"

"Sure," said the X-ray doctor, looking at his scraggly body with pity and expecting the tiny man to burst into tears. But Thay Phung just laughed out loud:

"It would be strange if I did not have a tumor! During five years in the jungle, the only water I drank came from below the layer of fallen leaves defoliated by the toxic spray from American planes. If I don't die from that, I wouldn't think much of the invader's technology!"

Thay Phung arrogantly awaited his impending death. But he did not die. Why? Because it was not the end of his fate. Because he was born in the year of the cat, and cats are famous for being long-lived! Because the X-ray doctor took the wrong patient's file, ironically one belonging to a fat colonel who had lived safely in the rear for years.

Not dead, Thay Phung, with his stature like a mistake from heaven, was sent back to his teaching career. After years fighting his own war in the jungle, he was old, weak, and quiet with peculiar ways more like an old man's than one of twenty-four.

When people give to beggars, they do it with a feeling of pity.

But once when he was eating sweet potatoes and an old beggar came to him for food, he invited the beggar inside, made him a bowl of instant noodles, and even thanked him when he left. People asked him why, and he said: "Because thanks to beggars, we have the chance to show our kindness." Looking at the principal of his school, he said, "Like you—you have your high position right now because we are stupid. In the land of blind, the one-eyed man rules. Thus, do not be self-conceited!"

In his room, the ceiling was full of cobwebs. The principal teased him: "Thay Phung wants the spiders to help him keep the environment clean, without flies and mosquitoes." He just pursed his lips, shaking his head and said: "Sadly watch the spider spinning webs. With this sublime line of poetry comes proof that not everything is done with self-interest!" When he went out, he wore his cap with the visor covering the scruff of his neck. He explained: "Remember to watch out for thieves from behind, and that, in this world, many people not born in the year of the horse are very good at kicking backward!"

No! He did not care that the principal's face darkened whenever he said things like this with a sneering tone. Though the principal did not seem to like him, his students loved and admired him because they knew how thoroughly responsible and sincere he was. They recognized the charm of his heart, his talent, and his erudition. Because when he gave lectures, he seemed to walk out of his skinny and sickly body, magically transforming into a charismatic and stately knight. His career gave him the chance to reveal his potential, to burn his lingering doubts. His eyes sparkled. His voice boomed. His movements fit his words. His new ideas, colorful metaphors, and funny euphemisms impressed his students. They felt very lucky—it was a happiness to come to his class! Students in other classes wanted to join his so much they cut their own to sneak in and listen to his lectures. This, among other things, made the other teachers very jealous.

Every course he taught was interesting, and in every subject, he demonstrated some extraordinary talent. He could draw a circle as round as if drawn with a compass. In geography, he could sketch a map with the borders as exact as a printed one. The specimen birds and cats he stuffed and the experiments he carried out in biology, physics, and chemistry also made the other teachers jealous. From his music class, he used his golden voice to create a singing movement within the whole school. Obviously he was a versatile talent, but he positively shone when teaching literature. One day, Thuy, one of his ninth-grade students, said to him honestly, "Please forgive me, Thay! Many times when listening to your poetry lectures, I keep feeling like I'm in a land of dreams." Eighteen years old, she had an oval face, black eyes as mysterious as a mountain girl's, and long hair that reached her waist. A fellow great lover of literature, she admired him very much. He told her: "Do not praise me, because listening well is much better than speaking well."

But where talent and virtue reside, so lurks jealousy. The principal, Thuc, was a dwarfishly small, mean and misshapen man who earned his promotions by slandering others. He had piggy eyes, hair thick as a horse's mane, and one leg shorter than the other. After high school and two more years at the teacher's training college, he still could not write full sentences or solve equations with one unknown, let alone differential, integral, or derivative equations! Socially, he was even worse: he neglected his work and spoke thoughtlessly. In fact, his only talents seemed to be envying and criticizing others, such as Thay Phung. Thuc castigated Thay Phung for the way he walked—which made him bob up and down—and for his graceful handwriting—which Thuc considered foppish. He ridiculed Thay Phung for having stood on tiptoe and eaten and drunk so much to enlist, only to be forgotten in a jungle ammo dump. But Thuc did not know living alone in the jungle gave Thay Phung a rare chance in life. One must be thoroughly individualized in the community. One must know right from wrong by oneself, not by accepting the word of others. One must be useful to other people. Fame did not matter! The five years fighting his own jungle war was an education more valuable than the five peaceful years of life in the rear enjoyed by quite a few other people!

In this world, people are not kind to one another! Or in Thay Phung's humorous words, "People don't like each other, they only like finding ways to hurt one another!" Was that so? There is still no answer to that question! Then came another turn in Thay Phung's life. At the end of that school year, teachers and students alike were astonished to learn about Thay Phung's downfall. Principal Thuc said sharply: "The inviolable student-teacher relationship must never be contaminated, but Thay Phung has had the audacity to write a love letter to his student, Thuy! Does he still deserve to work at our advanced school?"

But he did not have to end his career. He only had to move to Pao Mao Chai, a mountain village in a remote area of my province, a three-day walk away. It had two hamlets three kilometers away from each other. The children there had never had a school. The illiterate village officers could only sign by pressing their fingerprints on official documents or reports written or read for them.

Another five years passed after Thay Phung's exile to Pao Mao Chai. And another miracle happened, just as when he lived in the jungle. People could forget him, but they could never forget the work he had done. Not a single mortar out of place. In Pao Mao Chai, regardless of being unjustly punished, he helped the village build a primary school. Afterward, all the village officers could read and write. The school district even added a branch school in the other hamlet staffed by two volunteer female teachers.

He created that miracle. He was like a monk practicing all his life and then finally being rewarded. He could manage himself in difficult circumstances and follow his own way to reason without need for advice, solace, or even encouragement. Thay Phung had talent, skill, and spirit! A journalist of the province's newspaper happened to get lost in Pao Mao Chai, discovered him, and offered to write an article commending him as a people's hero. The reporter included many amazing stories. For example, in just three months, Thay Phung could speak the local H'mong language fluently and even sing traditional H'mong songs to entice students to come to class. Just about everyone, not just the students, loved his voice. He cleared land and planted corn to feed himself and help the poor students. He even erected a pole in the branch schoolyard where the two female teachers lived and worked so they could tie a white cloth on the pole whenever they needed help. Without telephones, Thay Phung told them, it was the quickest way to communicate. The only snag came the first time, when the teachers found themselves without a white cloth and, in a panic, strung up a pair of white panties!

Of course the article made a really strong impression. The province committee called the Ministry of Education: why not take Pao Mao Chai as a model to apply elsewhere? The ministry immediately assigned the provincial Office of Education to establish a delegation of inspectors to verify the stories in Pao Mao Chai. But heading the delegation was none other than Principal Thuc, who in the past five years had been promoted to chief of the office. When Thay Phung saw Thuc at Pao Mao Chai, he smiled and said, "When the pig in the shoulder pole basket comes to market, then in the other basket, the banana comes too." Thuc ignored him, saying nothing at all. Thay Phung continued, "So the Monkey King, though magical, could not get out of the palm of Buddha's hand, right?" Thuc still did not say anything. After the inspectors finished their work, just before leaving, Thuc came to see Phung, and snarled, "Hey, don't think so highly yourself! How dare you let the women hang their underwear on the flag pole as a signal to their lovers? How on earth could anyone consider you a hero?"

Principal Thuc did not threaten idly. Thay Phung had committed a serious crime! And silently, without explanation, he accepted being fired.

Strangely, he returned happily to the ordinary life of an ordinary laborer. He became a handy carpenter, making tables and chairs and other educational equipment for the primary schools and kindergartens back in town. Sometimes he'd be found wearing a broad-brimmed palm-leaf hat, sitting alone on some sidewalk, completely wrapped up in his carving and sawing, singing to himself and looking very pleasant and relaxed.

That was it. He really was pleasant and relaxed. Because he had been to a faraway land, he had been knowledgeable, and he had fulfilled his dream of being useful. He had experienced ups and downs. To him, life was like a big house with many small rooms, enough space for sadness and happiness, bitterness and sweetness all to reside at once. People needed time on their own, talking to themselves, singing to themselves, finding their own ways and judging their own failures.

That was it. Carpenter Phung hid his face under the broad-brimmed palm-leaf hat, day by day absorbed in his work, with the words of the familiar song on his lips:

Oh Mountain girl! My life is like a bird soaring quickly
through the clouds and sky of time.
Oh Mountain girl!

Then came the day when, while he was carving and singing at
the same time, someone suddenly called his name. He looked up
and saw a beautiful woman with an oval face, a big chignon, and
a mountain girl's mysterious black eyes step up to the sidewalk.
Bewildered, he watched the woman approach, take his hand, and
say clearly, "Thay Phung! I am Thuy, do you still remember me? I
listened to your lectures on poetry and was transported to a land of
dreams!" Sadly, he shook his head: "Maybe you've confused me with
someone else." A woman now, not to be put off, Thuy said, "No!
No! How could I mistake you?" Then she cried, "Everything was my
fault, Thay Phung!" and explained that a love letter she had written
to him while still his student was somehow found by Principal Thuc
and immediately became the cause for all his trouble. He carefully
listened to what Thuy said but then shook his head again, repeating,
"You've confused me with someone else." And again, the beautiful
woman named Thuy would not permit his deception. She took off
his hat and looked into his face and said, "Phung . . . your face . . .
your extraordinary talent! How can I be confused?" Still he denied
her, saying, "Thank you, but I have a twin brother who looks exactly
like me," but this time, tears ran all over his face, his entire body
shook, and like a miraculous answer to his most guarded prayers,
the beautiful woman Thuy put her head on his shoulder, sobbing,
"Phung! Now that we've found one another, don't ever hide from
me again!"

One's life, after all, is a very long road of seeking fulfillment. So
Thay Phung had finally arrived at his destination. He was special and
talented, and he had spirit. And the beautiful woman also arrived

at her destination by fulfilling her secret love with him. Sadly, their story does not end here. Five years being a soldier guarding a munitions depot in a jungle defoliated by Agent Orange could not simply fade into the past. It haunted him. This time, the X-ray doctor did not make a mistake with the file. A tumor as big as a guava had grown in his left lung. Nine of ten soldiers guarding the ten ammunition stockpiles in that jungle had already died from the poison the Americans sprayed. Would Thay Phung be the last to die? He shook his head, smiling: "I will not give up so easily!" Hearing him laugh at his fate this way, Thuy, now his wife, burst into tears.

Hanoi, 2002

TRANSLATED BY TRAN THI QUYNH HOA AND CHARLES WAUGH

LOVE FOREST

The news of Thinh's death from the Americans' toxic chemical poisoning, delivered by phone by the old H15 guys, knocked K'sor H'Guonl for a loop. For many years H'Guonl had kept living because of her love for Thinh. Now that he was dead, she dreamed of him every night.

She dreamt that Thinh was holding her, and just as her lips touched his, helicopter rotors would begin to whir and startle him into running away. She tried to run after him but her legs seemed to wind together so tightly she couldn't move. Then she'd wake, her legs stiff, and Thinh's spirit would disappear into the forest again. If H'Guonl could fall back asleep, back to her unfinished dream, she'd dream that Thinh was leading her along a shallow stream where dozens of colorful butterflies suddenly flew into the air, making H'Guonl's body feel so light that she herself rose up into the forest with them, leaving him alone, looking dazed. In another dream, Thinh sat on the outpost kitchen porch with a book, teaching her how to read Vietnamese. Suddenly, the words coming from his mouth turned into bees. They swarmed over her body, tickling her skin, making her want to scream. But her mouth was too numb to say anything. The scream, stuck deep down in her throat, would wake her up.

Other dreams returned her to the forest of their love. Once she saw Thinh carrying a heavy load up a slope, his shoulders lopsided under the weight. Suddenly the sky turned fiery as an American napalm attack sent flames curling everywhere. They engulfed Thinh; then he appeared writhing on the banks of the Ia Mo River. "Oh God, it can't be like this!" she shouted. "Jump in the river!"

Immediately, Thinh plunged into the water. When he surfaced near the place where H'Guonl sat on the riverbank, waiting for her rice to cook, the napalm had been reduced to the small fire beneath her ricepot, and a morning had just dawned. She smiled at him, and as he smiled back an American bomb suddenly exploded, throwing Thinh, H'Guonl, and all her pots and pans into the forest. Thinh began coughing terribly. His clothes had been blown off and he was flying over the fields where H'Guonl now stooped, picking pumpkin buds. American planes roared down at them, pouring a dusty, yellow rain. The toxic mist roiled all around them, engulfing Thinh entirely. Without a wet towel to cover his mouth, Thinh soon fell stone dead. H'Guonl cried and wailed. Thinh's stilt-like legs curled up. His dead, skinny arms tried to prop up H'Guonl so she could stand, but she would not rise.

In her dreams, they ran and ran again.

During the war, Thinh, a very tall man, had to carry cassava and firewood from the mountain fields just like everyone else in Unit H15, but the way he did it seemed really different to H'Guonl, and she liked that. She also liked the way he made studying how to write so easy. Even the way he spoke was unusual, but this too she found to be more charming than with other people.

Thinh's manner and attitude combined simplicity and leisureliness. Nevertheless—no one knew why—all the seemingly ordinary features of this particular man appealed to H'Guonl.

Maybe it was because the kitchen doors looked normal compared to everyone but Thinh because of his height. Each time he came in from the field, he had a hard time setting down the heavy back-basket. Then, wide-eyed, he carried the wood into the kitchen for her. Although she said nothing, she pitied him deeply. H'Guonl quietly arranged a place for him to unload the basket right next to the kitchen doors. She did not want Thinh to have to kneel when he set down his burden.

As for Thinh, unintentionally, he thought of her as a small child. He patted her head as if she were six years old. Moreover, he publicly praised her as a smart girl, forgetting that she had a husband and child already.

Whenever he returned from a mission, Thinh always had something for her. Once, he gave her a bracelet made of K'rac wood that he said he'd made when he had free time. After another mission, she received a comb made from the aluminum of a downed airplane. H'Guonl even received a necklace of tiny wooden beads. It was the prettiest string of beads she'd ever seen in her life. H'Guonl wondered how he could make such burnished and colorful beads from K'rac wood, which everyone else usually just threw away.

Thinh showed her his small drill and file—the two things he took with him everywhere—that had been passed down to him from previous generations. Thinh told her for him they were like the indispensable machete and back-basket that the J'Rai men always kept with them. "Not true!" Thinh said suddenly, correcting himself. "I mean the machete and crossbow."

"Also not true!" replied H'Guonl. "These days, the most indispensable things all J'Rai men carry are a machete and a rifle!"

After the Chu Mo campaign, seeing everyone return except Thinh, H'Guonl sat by the spring all morning, forgetting to prepare lunch for the unit. At noon, they found her sitting alone, crying. It turned out Thinh had not returned because he had gone out on a mission, not because he was dead. The news was a relief to her, but even so, on all previous missions he had sent some word to her, and sometimes even sent gifts for others to deliver to her.

When he did finally return, Thinh was a different man. He purposefully avoided her. He didn't dare give her gifts as before. Too sad for words, H'Guonl not only kept her silence but also refused to look at him. When someone teased Thinh and H'Guonl about one another, she showed complete indifference, and even when Thinh carried firewood and vegetables to her kitchen, she ignored him as if he were not important. One day, Thinh lingered near the fire in the kitchen drying his shirt, knowing she could not go out and leave her work. Waiting until they were alone, he asked, "Are you angry with me?"

H'Guonl did not respond. She stacked firewood. She poured water into a pot and began to cook cassava mash for the pigs. Forlorn, Thinh stepped out of the kitchen holding his ruined shirt. In the past, H'Guonl would have dried his shirt properly for him.

Everyone in the unit knew Thinh had not yet taken a wife. They also knew H'Guonl had a husband, Ko Pa Hieng, the chief of the district battalion. H'Guonl had fallen in love with Hieng for the refined way he carried himself when he came to her village to deploy troops during the campaign seasons. When she learned Hieng had been abandoned by a wife who couldn't bear the enemy's coercion tactics and ran off with a man from the other side, taking their two children with her, H'Guonl's love and compassion for him grew even more. It astonished the guerrillas of Plei Dit village to see H'Guonl entwined with Hieng. At first, H'Guonl and Hieng respectfully called each other Uncle and Child, but soon they used more intimate terms, and finally they had the nerve to embrace one another openly in public. H'Guonl's father and mother lived in a remote village, so they had no idea about them and could not intervene.

The whole district could hardly believe their distinguished leader had developed this unusual relationship with such a young and pretty female guerilla. "It's completely ordinary," said Hieng, when the party committee raised the issue of the morality of the chief's romantic affairs. "Besides," he added, "she loved me first."

They got married and had their first child, a son. With motherhood, H'Guonl became even more beautiful, more immune to the ravaging effects of war. Her skin became brighter. Her red lips became more gorgeous, more seductive, and more alive. She even sang ten times more beautifully than before. In the past, only a few people paid her any attention, but now no one could miss her as she transformed into a blooming woodland flower, unique among thousands of trees, sparkling to the eye.

Thus, the older, less attractive Hieng felt he had only two options: resign from his position as chief of the district armed forces and take his wife back to his village, or force H'Guonl to quit cooking for the guerrillas and return to her parents' home. Of course, he made her quit her job. Hieng's position as chief was too important to give up. But Hieng still could not stop feeling insecure about her since people in the district party committee, thinking such a capable woman should not be left at home doing nothing, suggested he should let her cook for them for a while, then go to school to study culture and, after that, medicine. That was the simple and orderly near future they envisioned. But after a few months with her at the district party office, Hieng felt even more insecure. Keeping her at home, no one dared to approach her due to his prestige, but at the district offices, there were a lot of guys who really knew how to talk. They rarely went out to the front, which meant they wouldn't die easily, and they were much better looking than the run-of-the-mill guys in the village. In short, Hieng could not focus on his work. Luckily, a new elite unit, H15, comprised entirely of Northerners, had just been posted to the area. Because they had received a high level of cultural training and had a stronger work ethic, more organizational discipline, and more heart than other units, Hieng believed he'd feel more secure assigning her there. He arranged with H15's chief officer, a man named Han who had a good sense of humor, to have H'Guonl join them as cook and logistical manager. H'Guonl hesitated at first, intending not to go. She wanted to know why she had to change jobs again after just getting used to the last one.

"It's your assignment," Hieng said, "you have to carry it out."

"And what about our little boy at home?"

"He has his grandparents, and he has me. I'll visit him once or twice a month."

"If I move to a different unit," said H'Guonl, "will you let me visit my son after a while?"

"Why not?"

H'Guonl lowered her head. "I miss him already."

"Working as a revolutionary fighter," said Hieng, folding his arms across his chest, "you should not talk about missing. Step-by-step, I'll handle everything."

He began to say that a lot: because she was a revolutionary fighter, she had to do this. Because she was a revolutionary fighter, she had to do that. As evidence, she had to be apart from her child, move to another unit, and follow the command's decision without question. But, in fact, he was the one who made the decision, and she knew it.

And although Hieng sent his wife to a very respectable unit with very respectable soldiers, he remained as insecure as ever. Hieng couldn't focus on his job when he began to imagine someone, somewhere, sneaking around trying to take his wife away. Northern soldiers were not just well-cultured and handsome, they were highly educated too. That was the truth. And H'Guonl was not the guerilla H'Guonl of the past. The regular uniform had turned her into a strong and beautiful woman. Her demeanor—in fact, her whole way of living—also changed. In her tent, she had a mirror, a comb, perfume, a vase of flowers, and even posters on the wall. She could speak Vietnamese fluently. Not only that, but the unit gave her the opportunity to study, and Hieng did not feel it was appropriate to ask his wife about her teacher. But always he felt haunted by suspicion.

As for H'Guonl, after she had met Thinh she could no longer see Hieng as handsome or as needing her compassion but only as a furious and growling predator who one day might eat her.

For a long time, every night that Hieng and H'Guonl spent together remained silent enough to hear the murmur of the brook, the sound of dry twigs dropping, wild animals smacking their tongues, and mosquitoes whining outside the nets. Hieng never said anything, drinking wine from his canteen for the flush of strength it gave him and no longer inviting her to join him as he used to. Then he would rush to her and tear off her clothes, not to ravish her, but to frantically shine a flashlight all over her body, looking for signs of infidelity. The first time, she thought he was teasing her, so she laughed and teased him back: "It must be musty already!" He growled in response but did not speak.

At last, one night, Hieng suddenly went completely crazy, jumping up and rushing from the tent into the pitch black outside. Then he rushed back in again. Without a sound, he held her tightly, making her feel cold and disgusted. She had never had such a feeling as that one before. He pawed at her body, grabbing and squeezing and using her roughly, like she was a body without soul.

Once. Twice. Three, four, maybe five nights this happened. After the last, he spoke to her weakly: "Am I your husband, H'Guonl?"

"No," she answered. "I'm not your wife anymore, Hieng. Divorce me!"

He shouted in J'Rai, "If you're not my wife, whose wife are you?"

"I'm nobody's wife!"

Hieng snatched his K59 from its scabbard.

"Killing me would be easy," H'Guonl said, "but who'll take care of our son? Let me go home to him."

The next morning, Hieng went to speak with Mr. Han, and the following afternoon he brought H'Guonl home. His worries should have been over: never again would H'Guonl be able to meet with the men from Unit H15.

The more jealous Hieng became, the more distant H'Guonl grew. The more he tried to control her, the more she did just to spite him. She even rejoined her old guerrilla unit, living at home in the village during the day and operating against the enemy at night. Just living together in the same village did not solve their problems; they still quarreled constantly, prompting Hieng to sacrifice a pig, praying to Jang to reconcile them.

After the sacrifice, Hieng returned to his district battalion to prepare for another Chu Mo campaign to be undertaken with all the guerrillas in the area, as well as Unit H15. Once they had the Chu Mo post, they could liberate all the areas surrounding Cheo Reo. Mr. Han assigned Thinh to a reconnaissance team. Hieng sent Pui Be, also from his hometown, to take the recon team to the village. There they met H'Guonl, who was just as surprised to see Thinh as he was to see her.

The first night, all the units came together; local guerrillas and regular army all as one stayed up late drinking the local rice wine from gourds with reed straws and eating delicious soups. Thinh let himself become quite drunk and stumbled back to his tent to sleep. H'Guonl brought him a bowl of chicken soup, continuing on as if they had a plan. As if all their comrades already knew about their love. Thinh kissed H'Guonl as he had never kissed anyone before. H'Guonl responded, kissing him too, falling headlong into his heart. All reason failed him, and her as well, as they wound themselves around each other. Suddenly, just as H'Guonl was ready to give herself entirely to him, Thinh shivered uncontrollably. He stood up, collected her clothes for her and hurriedly put on his own. Without saying a word, he ran into the forest.

The next day, Thinh's recon team also vanished into the forest, leading the campaign. H'Guonl never saw any of them again.

Now, both H'Guonl's two men were gone.

After divorcing H'Guonl, Hieng married one of the district nurses, had a daughter, and then both were killed during the last days of the Deo Gio campaign. When H'Guonl heard of their deaths, she asked the district to allow her to adopt Hieng's baby. She gave the baby a name from her family, Kor H'Lien.

Her son grew up to be a district chief, and Kor H'Lien a doctor at a provincial hospital. Knowing her mother's sad love story, H'Lien and her husband took the train with H'Guonl to Thanh Hoa to attend the ceremony for the first anniversary of Thinh's death. Thinh's stick-thin wife did not look capable of bearing the burden of two feeble-minded and deformed children unable to do anything for themselves. Brushing away her tears, H'Guonl told her children to give Thinh's family her retirement pension book and wounded soldier aid book. She would help Mrs. Thinh carry her burden over the love forest's final slope, heavy as it was.

Hanoi, 2005

TRANSLATED BY TRAN THI QUYNH HOA AND CHARLES WAUGH

NGUYEN THI NGOC HA

THE SPIRIT POND

The girl who helped with my cooking and cleaning looked anxious when she opened the gate and said hello. "Maybe something serious has happened with your family," she said. "Your uncle has phoned so many times, and he just called again. He said if I saw you come home from work to tell you you've got to go out there as soon as possible."

My paternal grandparents had three children. Their eldest daughter, my aunt Ca Mau, went to work in a fishing village near the Tien Hai district at a very young age. Then they had my father, and eleven years later, my uncle Doan. My grandfather died before Doan's first birthday. My grandmother worked very hard to raise her boys and to make sure they stayed in school.

My father also died when I was still very young. Since Aunt Ca Mau had taken a husband in the fishing village, and since my grandmother allowed my mother to marry a new husband when I was five, Grandma and Uncle Doan raised me as their own child, taking care of me with love. Uncle Doan felt things deeply but learned to hide his bitterness and sorrow in silence. When he did choose to communicate with people, he always made a good impression, coming across as a fluent and joyful person. He also had a good sense of humor and liked to help other people. Because he always treated people straightforwardly and honestly, his business deals didn't always work out the best for him, which put him somewhat at a disadvantage nearly all his life.

I treated Doan as my father, even though he was only twelve years older than me. Whenever I earned good grades, he made a clay animal figurine for me as a reward. Anywhere he went, he let me come along. In later years, when I moved up to level three and had to go to the district school all week, I could only come home on weekends. How I missed my uncle then! At the start of each new week, when it was time to leave home again, I could hardly bring myself to take half a step.

In December 1967, before finishing high school, Doan joined the army. For the first two years, he sent letters home regularly, always including a private letter for me. But after that, we didn't hear anything from him for a long time. My grandma got sick, she was so sad. Despite it all, she forced herself out of bed every day hoping my uncle would return, not wanting to be caught having given up.

Sorrow settled like a black cloud over my family. Grandma's illness worsened to the point she felt it necessary to call my Aunt Ca Mau to her side. "I know I won't get any better," she said. "When I die, I want you to pray for me at the temple and at the spirit pond afterward. Pray also for Doan to come home safely. When he does, take a wife for him, so he can give birth to a child who will continue to honor our ancestors." Silently I prayed that Grandma would live to see my uncle's return.

She died still waiting for her son, just two weeks before the liberation of the South.

Hearing of Grandma's death, Aunt Ca Mau came home right away to pray with me at the temple and spirit pond as her mother had wished. Many soldiers began to come back from the front, and the deaths of many others were reported to their families, but even six or seven months after Unification Day, we still had not heard a word about my uncle.

In October of the following year, two pieces of good news came at the same time. The first was I had been accepted into the College of Education; the second was that my uncle was still alive and under medical treatment at the military hospital in Hai Duong. I was so happy! My body trembled, shivering with sweat. I rushed home and placed the letters on the altar. Standing in front of the pictures of my grandma and father, I didn't know how to pray; my voice was too choked by tears.

By evening, everyone was as merry as at Tet. The next morning, several of my great aunts and uncles and second cousins joined Aunt Ca Mau and me in going to see my uncle. We were all happy, me most of all. I wished I was still a small child so I could hug my uncle, sit on his lap, and ask him to tell me his stories of the war. But when I saw him, I felt so strange I couldn't speak or ask him anything. I just cried. A terrible pain had bloomed from my heart and stuck in my throat. Before going to war, Doan was one of the most handsome men in our village, slender in build, with a wide forehead circled by thick and wavy black hair. The features of his face came together in a harmonious and manly way. But where had that man gone? The man sitting on the bed seemed a stranger, his face pale and skeletal, his mouth deformed by a long scar that cut through his chin. Only his big, sharp eyes and sonorous voice had not changed, confirming the stranger really was Uncle. He looked at me and said:

"Oh my goodness! My niece has become a young lady, already more charming than the big-city girls. You have no idea how often I've thought about you while sitting alone in some foxhole between battles, imagining how you've grown up, worrying each time news came around about American bombs falling on schools. It never mattered if it was in our district or not."

I wanted so badly to reprimand him for not writing to us for so long, but I couldn't with everyone else there asking questions. He knew we avoided mentioning his losses. His eyes glistened with tears and gradually turned red, looking at everybody, then settling on Aunt Ca Mau. In a low voice, he said, "I feel guilty about Ma. I'm very sorry for not having sent letters home, but for all these last years I had been given a secret assignment. I wasn't allowed to contact our family. In '73, a comrade was sent north for training, and I asked him secretly to take a message to Ma and all of you, but he never made it. After the liberation of the South, everyone was so excited, preparing to return home to see our families, but instead my unit received orders to march to the Cambodian border. Only when wounded was I demobilized. The doctors are taking some days to stabilize me first, then they'll remove the shrapnel from behind my left lung."

After a short time, the doctors moved him to Hospital 108. There, the doctors decided operating might be more dangerous than leaving the shrapnel where it was. When Doan came home, the government rewarded his service by appointing him head of our agricultural cooperative.

March not yet past, the flowers had fallen from the kapoks and scattered below, the petals like splendid red lanterns shining on the land. The fresh, green spring paddy by the road wavered in the wind like enormous bolts of brilliant green silk.

Absorbed by my thoughts, I didn't realize at first that I'd reached the great banyan tree that marked the top of the village. When I was a child, five or six of us holding hands still couldn't reach all the way around its gnarly, twisting trunk. Its luxuriant canopy shaded the roof of a temple built on the bank of a large pond that has been there forever, through droughts and storms, generation after generation, unchangeable. Whenever I walked by that pond, I always felt its sacred and mysterious majesty. When I was a child, sometimes my grandma or Uncle Doan would take me the ten kilometers to

Aunt Ca Mau's house by the sea, and we would have to pass by the pond. Overgrown with weeds, it attracted many flocks of wild ducks searching for food. If we made a sound, the ducks would fly up into the air together, the wind from their wings rushing like the sound of a waterfall, beating down the grass and rippling the surface of the water. Once, Grandma told me its story:

"Spirits of the dead of this area often gather round the pond. On the night of the thirtieth of every month, anyone walking by would see several tiny round boats and many lanterns floating on the water. The wind begins to blow, wailing through the casuarina on the mound above the pond. Sometimes it seems that someone is weeping loudly. I don't know what happened long ago in the past, but when I was a young girl, I saw some people drown themselves in the pond. Since then, no one dares to pass this area alone at night. No one's ever seen a ghost, so no one knows what one looks like, but even so, a long time ago, our ancestors named this place the spirit pond. People came to believe that villagers who pray on the fifteenth of July each year for the spirit at the temple and for the souls of people who died unjustly will be very lucky in life and business."

Uncle Doan said worshipping ghosts was pure superstition. Once, he told Grandma: "You should pray to the spirit of the temple for a safe life without calamity, for a good harvest for the whole village, and for a good education for all the children. If you pray for all of us to have good lives, no one will ever become the ghosts you think wander around here, haunting all our good days. You shouldn't be kneeling down alone around the pond for all this mystical business."

At any rate, the pond remained, and the huge banyan tree and Ha village remained. Only human beings of various generations disappeared quietly from the earth. No one from grandma's generation was still alive. Some people from Uncle Doan's generation also passed away. In my generation, a few people like me had been lucky enough to receive a good education. Everyone else had to earn their living with their own sweat. After the Renovation, many villagers tried very hard to make a go of some kind of business; a few made fortunes somewhere far from home. But more commonly, many returned home after losing a lot of money.

Seeing so many go far away, fail, and have to return, my uncle decided to try to make his fortune at home in the village. He persuaded the district leaders to allow him to raise fish in the spirit pond. No one in our family supported this decision except me, since I thought it was a good investment. He borrowed some money from the Agriculture Encouragement Association, some from his former comrades, and a considerable amount from me.

He threw himself into the work, hiring workers to dredge the pond bed, grade the banks, and clean up the area. He also bought more casuarinas to plant around the pond and worked very hard all day and night.

After nearly a week, the pond was ready. Uncle Doan bought the best fish breeding stock from a fish-farming company in the district and consulted with aquacultural technicians about how to produce the highest yields. He hired Aunt Ca Mau's two sons, my cousins, to keep watch over the pond.

Uncle Doan's hard work paid off. In just a short time, he transformed the desolate landscape around the pond into a beautiful place. It seemed the ghosts had disappeared, and the wind didn't sound so mournful and fierce as the days before. The blue sky and clouds framed in the reflection off the pond were like a giant picture.

The villagers who passed the pond admired Uncle Doan's work. They said: "This veteran is something else! He really walks the talk and knows where he's going!"

Uncle Doan's project made good progress. The fish grew big and heavy. But suddenly, on the thirteenth of July, a typhoon blew into our province, driving rain all day and night before it. Several houses in the village lost their roofs, and others were pounded flat. Limbs and trunks from broken trees had been strewn everywhere. The village elders said such a big storm had never been seen before. The storm blew the water from the pond in waves and swept away all the fish.

I rushed to the village afterward to try to help. Uncle Doan had fallen apart like a withered leaf. Had the ghosts decided to punish him for not worshipping at the temple? I rejected the idea at once. At this moment the most important thing was to comfort and encourage him to overcome his sadness.

"Don't be sad, Uncle!" I said. "You will have better luck next time. Heaven would not wish people like you any harm."

He shook his head.

After this disaster, Uncle Doan accepted his loss and transferred his business to the Youth Union. He threw himself into his work for the agricultural co-op, helping other people, and into raising his family. Now I wondered what else must have happened that he had so frantically asked me to come. When I came to the gate, I tried to keep calm. One of my cousins cheered from the yard: "Ly is coming!"

A lot of people were working busily in the garden. I asked the man who came to unlock the gate, "What's going on here? Where is my uncle?"

"I'm right here," said Uncle Doan, coming out of the house. "I'm glad you made it home in time."

What has happened to him this time? I wondered.

My sixty-year-old uncle looked like a man of more than seventy. Thin and shriveled, he had nothing left from his youth. Even his eyes and voice had changed. His eyes had sunk deep into his very high cheek-bones. His complexion had darkened. His once dense and manly head of hair had become sparse, even bare. When he spoke, his hoarse voice trembled. I turned my face to try to hide my worry about him and asked about something other than what I was thinking:

"Where is my aunt? Has she found anything to help with her arthritis?"

"No, in fact it seems worse than last year. Ask her yourself; she's helping Toan take a bath."

I looked toward the house without moving. He could tell I was worried about what was going on and said, "Tinh has gone to town with some of her friends to rent a wedding dress."

"Who's getting married?"

"Oh! Tinh, of course."

"Why didn't you tell me last time? Or on the phone?"

"Your aunts and I decided it just a few weeks ago," said Uncle Doan. "I've called a dozen times to tell you, but you're never home."

Through the kitchen window, I could see some women busy cooking for the wedding. They really were going to do it. A wedding out of the blue was a huge surprise, but I found myself sighing with relief. It could be worse.

Within a year of being demobilized, my Uncle Doan took a wife, Le, who was the sister of one of his army buddies from Nho Quan. She was a healthy and charming, if not exactly beautiful, woman.

They gave birth to a pretty daughter with a light complexion and named her Tinh. Everyone said Aunt Ca Mau's ceremonial worship of the ghosts had finally paid off. Smiling, Aunt Ca Mau said, "It's good to have a daughter as a first child. Next year, maybe you'll have a son as a gift from the spirits of the pond."

Uncle Doan looked excited and joyful. On the little girl's one-month birthday, he and Aunt Le invited all their relatives to a feast to celebrate the health of the baby. The room went silent after Uncle Doan called for everyone's attention. "Thank you all for coming to celebrate the good health of my wife and daughter," he said, raising his glass. "And now that my great anxiety of so many years has passed, may I ask you now to toast my happiness?" Uncle Doan passed his gaze from silent face to silent face and continued slowly: "Once, my unit passed through a vast and ancient forest in Tay Ninh Province. It had become a 'forest of the dead,' the trees and bushes and grass all withered. Not a single bird sang all day. All the boulders in the stream were covered with a powdery gray dust." Uncle Doan's hand trembled, spilling his wine. He set it down, pausing for another moment. "From my company, most of my comrades did not survive the war, and all of those who did, except me, have been affected by dioxin."

"Don't talk much about the war, please," interrupted Aunt Ca Mau. "Let's remember the present, and toast your family's happiness."

Aunt Le gave birth to another child at the end of the following year. Not a son, as predicted, but a daughter, very similar to Tinh, except she had no bones in her legs. Uncle Doan sank into depression. Everyone told my uncle, don't try to have any more children; remember the Agent Orange. But Uncle Doan persisted, saying to Aunt Ca Mau, "Tinh has grown up in very good health, so how can I be affected by Agent Orange? Maybe while Le carried Toan, she had a bad cold or fever but didn't think it was serious." When Tinh turned five, Le gave birth to a third child. This time, it was a boy, but he was so terribly deformed he died just after being born.

Uncle Doan tried to keep calm when comforting Le. He didn't want anyone to know the anguish hidden deep in his mind and soul. Only when alone with me did he weep as bitterly as a child. All my life, I have never been able to stand to see a man cry, especially not my uncle, and those tears fell so heavily to the ground I can still feel their weight, even today.

Time curled past like in everyone's life. Yet these invisible and brutal ghosts continued to haunt my family. It made me angry, and I wished for some extraordinary power to fight back against the ghosts, to chop them to pieces or burn them to ashes. But in fact, I could do nothing to ghosts that had invaded the blood and cells of my uncle's and cousins' bodies. Uncle Doan and his family had no choice but to go on living their difficult life, every day just like the one before. Soon Toan was twenty-two, still lying motionless on the bed, as small as a seven-year-old.

"Ly!" Aunt Le called to me from the kitchen. "Come take a bath to cool off. We'll make an offering to the ancestors after that. The groom and his family are coming to take Tinh at the hour of the goat."

The sound of girls' voices flittered outside the gate. Seeing that I'd come home, Tinh rushed right to me and took my hand. "It's so lucky you made it for the wedding!"

"I had no idea you were getting married," I said. "I only came because I was worried about all of you. Look—I brought vitamins and milk, not a wedding gift. Why did you keep it a secret from me? I don't even know the groom."

Tinh withdrew her hand from mine and ran inside crying.

By this time, Tinh was twenty-four, nearly five feet four and with a shapely figure. Her eyes were round and black, and her hair thick and sleek like her father's in his youth. Even though she was so often sad, her face became radiant when she smiled, and despite working in the fields each day, her complexion remained clear and bright. She and I could be mistaken for sisters, though she was much more charming and attractive.

After lunch, I learned that Tinh was supposed to become the second wife of a man in Thuong village. Much older than Uncle Doan, he already had three daughters, two of whom were older than Tinh. Listening to all this, I exploded. "Heaven and earth! How can you make such a rash decision for your own child? It's not only against the law but an abomination!"

Everyone kept silent. Doan smoked his pipe, every now and then coughing convulsively, sounding like the ploughshare breaking up a stony field.

Aunt Ca Mau quietly broke the silence. "Several women in our village have become second wives. They didn't have to register the marriage. It's all right if the two families have reached an agreement. They only have to pay a fine when they apply for a birth certificate for a newborn child."

"Our family doesn't have to go around offering our own children to pay our debts," I said indignantly. "Tinh is a pretty and charming woman; she doesn't have to be a second wife. That would be fine if the man's wife was already dead or they had divorced. No! I don't agree with you. When they come to take her, I'll make them see how wrong this is. And I'll pay his expenses for the wedding. After that, I can take Tinh to the city for seamstress training. I'll find her a good job in the city, and she can get married later."

I heard Tinh sobbing in the other room. Aunt Le took my hand and asked me gently to calm down. "Don't be upset, sweetheart, it's just not as easy as you think. After twenty, most people in the village think girls are too old for marriage. All the young men have already married, and the ones who leave to work in the city don't like marrying country women. You know several girls Tinh's age went to work in the city and ended up selling themselves?"

I persisted: "A few years ago, two or three boys asked to marry her—why didn't you accept?"

My uncle finally broke his silence. He breathed hard, his voice hoarse. He wouldn't look at anyone directly, just the blank space in front of him, as though in that space were the terrible things causing him and his family so much pain and suffering. "Some years ago, several boys did say they wanted to marry Tinh, but they changed their minds after thinking about Tinh inheriting my blood and possibly giving birth to a deformed child. Fortunately this man from Thuong village doesn't care if he has more kids or not. Besides, it was his wife who came to propose. None of us believe this woman would mistreat Tinh. And it would be good for Tinh to work in his shop. That's much better than working the fields under the hot sun all day."

"She would be a servant, not a wife!" I cried. "Tinh can't possibly have agreed to this."

"She didn't. Not at first. But your aunt and I discussed it with her for a long time and finally convinced her."

As I listened to what they told me, my eyes filled with tears, my throat choked with pain, and my head spun. I ran out of the house to the meadow between the temple and the banyan tree that cast its shadow over the pond. I sat in the grass, covered my face with my hands, and sobbed. I wept for my small native village, for my uncle and his wife, for my poor cousin, and for the distress of my villagers. Tears poured from my eyes into the earth.

A cold wind blew from the sea and, with my tears, brought a bitter and salty taste to my lips. Beyond the temple, the wind whipped up waves on the pond that followed each other, crashing to the shore like the beats of a broken drum. Shadows from the casuarinas and the banyan rippled on the water surface. The glistening sunshine and the shadows of the trees and clouds on the waves created innumerable strange and miraculous visions. How can these ghosts appear during the day, I wondered. One, two, three, and then countless deformed bodies appeared, looking like my cousin Toan and the other specimens I'd seen at the Agent Orange medical research center in the city. Floating on the pond's surface, it seemed they were shouting and yelling. Suddenly I saw Toan's lovely face bob up in the water, then sink down again. "Oh!" I exclaimed. "You have no legs, cousin! How can you swim?" The deformed bodies began leaping from the water into the air where they transformed into a swarm of huge dragonflies above the pond. A second later, the dragonflies morphed into a squadron of American planes. Clouds of mist sprayed out from the planes, settling on the pond, turning it dark and hazy.

"Help! Help me!" I cried. "Agent Orange is killing me! It's killing everyone!"

"Ly! Wake up, honey."

My uncle's voice. He stood over me, shaking me by the shoulders. "It's weird you're having a nightmare during the day."

I sat up in the grass and wiped my eyes with one hand, trying also to wipe away the images from my dream.

"Maybe you remember all those stories about ghosts. Forget them! They're not true. Please don't cry any more. Your tears hurt your aunt and cousins and me more than you know. Tinh can have a husband right now and with luck might have a normal baby. Let's go home. They're just about to take the bride home now."

The place by the pond resounded with his voice, the sound of the wind, and the trembling leaves, and I knew the wind couldn't change anything else.

The dark clouds curled across the sky like an immense black curtain, closing it off into the dark. Big rain drops spattered down, pooling in the hollows of the brick courtyard. The crash of waves rolled in and out.

I sat at one corner of the bed with my hands between my knees, feeling lost with all the preparations in the house, not caring about the girls going here and there, helping Tinh with her dress and make-up in the room. Miserable with the idea that it would all be over soon, I just wanted to get out of the house, to escape, but I didn't because I knew if I left my uncle would be crushed.

The rain finally let up. A dim light sparkled behind the clouds. The muggy atmosphere was hard to bear, threatening a heavy rain later.

Right at two, a pack of men rode secondhand motorbikes into the courtyard. Leading the way, wearing a new suit, the heavily built groom had rough, red skin like a fighting cock. I stared at him with contempt and disgust.

This guy hadn't even finished fourth grade at the village school and wrote as scrawly as a kid just learning the alphabet. If he needed a letter or application written, he always asked his kids or others to do it, and even though his name was "Tac" he always signed his name by writing a "V" instead of a "T." This was the type of thing he could never master. Several generations of his family had been butchers, so for him, work and conversation alike were nothing but knives and cleavers. Some years ago, when a business dispute arose between him and his brother, the two of them chased each other up and down the lane with cleavers in hand. The brother had nearly been killed.

My uncle and the butcher were very different, but their desires converged in changing the fate of a young woman. My uncle tried his family's luck by risking the fate of his daughter because he hoped she would become a happy mother. Meanwhile, even though the butcher knew polygamy was illegal, he had an appetite for a second wife. Could Tinh manage to give birth to a healthy child? And I thought, child or no, she would never have a peaceful and happy life as a second wife, let alone with such a family.

The gate made of bamboo stood ajar, all the guests gone, my cousin taken by the butcher. Inside the house, my uncle lay motionless on his bed, my aunt sat in the kitchen with her arms wrapped around her knees, and I stood alone in front of our family altar. The incense sticks had burnt to the nub. Outside, rain poured down in torrents. Thunder boomed all around, the flashes of lightning like swords cutting the sky. Through the sound of the wind and the rain, I heard the cries of the ghosts wandering on the pond, and I feared for the nightmare that would haunt my sleep that night.

Hanoi, 2009

TRANSLATED BY CHARLES WAUGH AND HUY LIEN

MINH CHUYEN

A FATHER AND HIS CHILDREN

As a reporter for a newspaper in Nam Dinh Province, I was sent to visit Tran Van Ngo's family at seventh hamlet, Quang Minh Commune, to gather materials for a survey on the poor condition of veterans and their families who suffered illnesses caused by the war.

Mr. Ngo came back from the war thirty years ago. Nineteen years on the battlefield and he was never wounded, not even once. He always said his fate must be a great one since even during fierce fighting no bullet had ever hit him. After leaving the army, he worked hard in the fields from early morning to late evening. Then he got married and like most people hoped to have some children. But with the appearance of his first child a never-ending series of disasters began for his family.

After giving birth the first time, Mrs. Cam, his wife, cried out in terror at the monstrosity that came from her body. The child had bristly, black skin, a very short neck, and a big, elongated head. Mr. Ngo named him Tran Van Nhan. He died at the age of five.

After Mrs. Cam's second pregnancy, she gave birth to twins, a girl and a boy. The boy seemed normal, but the girl had black and ash-colored skin and dense, bear-like hair on her back and neck. To commemorate his nineteen years of fighting in the Tay Nguyen central highland region, Mr. Ngo named his son Tran Cao Nguyen. For his daughter he chose the name Thuy (primitive one) since the villagers said she resembled an ape-man.

Despite Tran Cao Nguyen's normal physical appearance, at the age of ten, he began to seem very odd. His face went slack, and he became frightened by bright light. During the night he would no longer sleep inside the house. Sometimes he slept in the peony bush; sometimes he would climb into a drinking-water tank.

Compared to Nguyen, Thuy suffered even more. She had lesions all over her black, hairy belly and would often have a high fever, during which she would lie on the bed, weeping and groaning.

Ngo and his wife borrowed money from their relatives to take their son and daughter to the hospital for treatment, but the doctors could not help Nguyen and Thuy.

Despite the lesions, mottled skin, and bristly hair, Thuy otherwise had a young girl's normal features. Her brilliant black eyes sparkled from her hairy face, and her long and smooth black hair shone brightly on her head.

Nguyen grew up to be a very quiet young man. He neither laughed nor raised his voice in anger. He never slept at night; instead, he sat up singing bits and pieces of various songs in a sad way. Mr. Ngo told me the story of arranging his marriage.

"When Nguyen turned twenty, I said to him: 'Nguyen! You have grown up now. Would you like to take a wife? Your mother and I will ask for a girl's hand for you.' He looked bewildered and said nothing. His strange eyes revealed only hatred, anger, and insanity. One month later, Nguyen seemed to be better, so I said: 'You are a young man now, you need to marry a wife and look ahead to a better future.' Nguyen nodded his head. After a short time, my wife and I arranged for Nguyen to marry Nguyen Thi Lan, a girl from a neighboring village.

"Marriage seemed to suit Nguyen; he began sometimes to like to talk and became sympathetic toward his wife and family. We were very happy for that.

"When Lan became pregnant, my wife was very pleased. She desperately wanted a grandson to continue our family line. I, on the other hand, felt a mixture of happiness and concern. I had heard of a veteran who had been affected by Agent Orange living in Ha Tay Province who had given birth to a son with some kind of mental illness. When his condition seemed to improve, his son got married and gave birth to a deformed child with two heads connected together. Three generations ruined by Agent Orange!

"Comparing that veteran's situation and mine, I had a premonition of the invisible disaster hidden inside the body of my daughter-in-law. When Lan saw 'the little thing' she gave birth to, she collapsed on the bed. The boy looked like my first child from twenty years ago. He had very short legs and a huge head. He differed from his uncle in that he had four eyes in his hairy face, and he only survived for three days."

Mr. Ngo nodded toward the baby in his arms. "This is Lan's second son, Linh," he said. "He's one now. A few days after his birth, his head began to retract like a turtle's. His arms and legs curved, and his neck became as stiff as a wooden rod. He must have pain in his body and limbs. He weeps and groans all day."

Mr. Ngo told me how the situation of Nguyen's little family had deteriorated over time. Nguyen's dioxin-related symptoms had gotten worse, manifesting themselves physically. "Sometimes, Nguyen's eyes tear up when his son shakes so violently and painfully. But most of the time, he doesn't seem to care what's happening around him, and sometimes he just laughs to himself helplessly."

"Where is Nguyen," I asked. "I'd like to see him."

"There," said Mr. Ngo, pointing to a white-haired, shrivel-faced old man who leaned against a column by the side of the front door. "That is my son. As you can see, he looks seventy years old, but he is only twenty-three."

"Uncle Ngo, can you tell me when and where you were poisoned?"

"On October 2, 1970, when my troops were garrisoned in a forest in Quang Da district, many American planes flew past dropping bombs; then they sprayed Agent Orange all over the forest. I hurt my right hand diving for cover, though not seriously, but suffocated under the chemicals. Many others also survived the bombing, but when the poison settled in, everyone had to go to the hospital for treatment. Several days later, when my comrades-in-arms came to see me, they said the trees that had been sprayed were stripped bare, their leaves withered and fallen. We had to abandon the area. Now many people from my unit have come home from military service sick or dying, and some have even passed their problems on to their children and grandchildren."

Mr. Ngo paused, his face looking very sad. Then he opened a tin box, took out some papers to show me and said:

"I have just written a letter to the director of the Monsanto Chemical Company in America that produced the toxic chemicals used in Vietnam. I urged him to compensate the victims affected by Agent Orange. Please read it and tell me what you think. It took a long time for my nephew in Hanoi to find the name of the director."

I read Mr. Ngo's letter:

Dear Mr. Shapiro:

Do you know the effects of the toxic chemicals your company produced to clear the forest and destroy the VC during the war? They not only devastated millions of hectares of jungle in the south of Vietnam, but also millions of Vietnamese people, including me, my children, and grandchildren. In the past thirty years, these toxic chemicals have wrought a horrible disaster. Hundreds of thousands of people affected by them have died an early death or are only half-alive. Deadly diseases, such as poliomyelitis, cancer, birth defects, blindness, and dumbness have passed from generation to generation. These are self-evident truths. But since the end of the American War, you and your company have not concerned yourselves with these effects. As the victims of Agent Orange's dioxin, we cannot stretch out on our deathbeds. We urge you to bear full responsibility for the use of toxic chemicals in Vietnam and compensate my family and the millions of families fallen victim to Agent Orange for the loss of their health and lives.

While Mr. Ngo and I discussed the letter, Nguyen came into the living room and yanked Linh from Mr. Ngo's arms. Grinding his teeth with anger, he nearly threw the little boy to the floor, but Mr. Ngo and I stopped him just in time. Gently, Mr. Ngo took the boy from Nguyen, who became so angry he threw a tea tray from the table to the floor.

He stared at Mr. Ngo and said. "I give the little bastard back to you. It's you who's made him so miserable."

"The baby suffers so much pain and misery already," exclaimed Mr. Ngo, "and now his father's gone crazy!"

"Yes, I'm crazy, you're crazy, and my son will be crazy. But why? Why is our whole family crazy? Why have we all suffered so much pain for so many years?"

Mr. Ngo wept bitterly. "Nguyen," he said, "the Americans have caused our pain and suffering. They sprayed toxic chemicals on our land and forest, and because the chemicals affected me, I passed their effects to you and you passed them to your son."

Witnessing three generations of this family's suffering, I couldn't find the right thing to say to Mr. Ngo to help calm him down. No words alone could ease their pain. It seemed better to keep my silence.

Three years later, after attending a conference on improving the medical care and living conditions of Agent Orange victims, I had another opportunity to visit Mr. Ngo's family.

Before I saw Mr. Ngo and Mrs. Cam, one of their neighbors told me the family had some bad luck recently: Nguyen had run away and was begging on the streets in Saigon. Mr. Ngo told me since they didn't have enough money to go find him they had no idea whether their son was still alive.

After Nguyen ran away, the situation of Mr. Ngo's family deteriorated. Thuy's illness became more serious as the lesions on her body swelled and bled, constantly soaking her clothes with blood. Sometimes she had a high fever and convulsions. Nguyen's son, Linh, had writhed on the bed, sobbing for more than a month, and now he could only whine in a low voice. He developed an intense fear of any kind of light, so whenever he could he would crawl quietly under the bed or lie with his face on the ground.

Because Mr. Ngo and his wife had a big family with sick kids to raise, they had fallen on extremely hard times. Ngo did not qualify as an injured pensioner since there was no aid policy for Agent Orange victims right after the war. Only recently, he and his daughter and grandson began to receive a small pension of about two hundred thousand dong per month—just enough for some injections to help control Thuy's convulsions. Because the medical treatments cost so much, they had to sell all their valuables at the market, and during moments of crisis, they had to borrow money at outrageous rates.

"Once," said Mr. Ngo, "I had nearly made up my mind to carry Linh on my back to the market to beg for our living. I thought, with his deformities, maybe people would pity him. But then I couldn't do it. I couldn't say to people walking by: 'May I beg a favor of you to help us. I was a soldier who went to war and was affected by Agent Orange. I passed my illness to my children and grandchildren. That's why we're having such a hard time.' Saying such a thing would be too shameful, especially as a veteran. So I have not become a beggar yet."

The other day, I came to visit Mr. Ngo's family and found them very busy. Thuy sat stripped to her waist while Mrs. Cam trimmed the hair covering her ulcerated skin. Whenever Thuy cried out, Mr. Ngo's face twisted with pain. At the same time, Linh lay with his face on the floor and began to convulse. Mr. Ngo immediately dropped to the floor to hold Linh's head. After ten minutes, the convulsions finally stopped, and Linh lay motionless on the floor, breathing hard and his body glistening with sweat.

This particular bout of illness had been getting worse for nearly a month, but Mr. Ngo and his wife didn't have the money to take Thuy or Linh to the hospital. Still owing their relatives and neighbors money, they felt they could no longer ask for help. Mr. Ngo asked Mrs. Cam to look for something in the wardrobe that might be worth some money. After a few minutes of searching, Mrs. Cam said, "Nothing's worth a penny in this house, except some of your medals."

"That's good! How could I forget them?" said Mr. Ngo. "I will take them to the market. Many people like to use the medals for decoration now."

"No," I said, "how can you do that? The medals show your glorious achievements in the war."

"Of course, I know that. They are my pride, and I don't want to lose them. But I have to sacrifice myself to save our children."

The next morning, Mr. Ngo filled a basket with five national medals and three medals for "Winning the American War," awarded for distinguished achievement, and walked slowly to the La market. He sat on the ground near some women selling rice. Several customers stared at his "special items" and felt compelled to chat with him.

"You've exchanged blood and tears for these medals, why sell them?" asked a farmer.

"Maybe they don't belong to him," said another man, laughing. "Maybe he's stolen them, so he's afraid of being laughed at if he wears them. Selling them is the best way for him."

Mr. Ngo sat quietly, not caring what they said. He remembered what a friend had told him: "You have to sell them to veterans who didn't earn any medals and have now become state employees or cadres who need medals to highlight their reputation for quick promotion."

Mr. Ngo waited patiently for these special customers. But no important employees came to this quiet village market, so Ngo waited in vain all morning. He finally went home thinking of going to the district market next time.

Mr. Ngo's home sat just one kilometer from the market, but after such a long day, it seemed to Mr. Ngo that he didn't walk with his own two legs. He staggered along until suddenly a flare of red and blue circles filled his eyes. The two rows of trees seemed to vibrate and bend over the road and the green leaves turned red. The purple water hyacinths also appeared to turn red. Even the sandy road became a resplendently pink strip of land. He had the amazing feeling that his feet no longer touched the earth but instead seemed to float on the air. Then he tumbled into the cold water.

Some farmers returning from the market jumped down into the pond and carried him back up to the road. They gave him mouth-to-mouth resuscitation, and turned his head to let him gag up the water from his lungs. Then they took him to a nearby infirmary.

After that day, Ngo's eyesight deteriorated, and he could no longer see his grandchildren writhing in pain or his wife washing the bloody ulcers on his daughter's body. But still he heard their heartrending moans and cries.

The Agent Orange victims in many areas began submitting complaints against the American chemical companies for compensation. Pham Hoang, the president of the Veterans Association of Quang Minh Commune, heard that Mr. Ngo had written a letter of complaint but did not want to send it to America. Hoang came to see Mr. Ngo and encouraged him to join the lawsuit against the companies that had provided the toxic chemicals to the American military. But Mr. Ngo said:

"Mr. Hoang, I have made up my mind, I don't want to send my letter to the American judge."

"Why not? Three generations of your family have suffered because of Agent Orange. How can you forgive those who did your family such harm?"

"It's true, my family has suffered," said Mr. Ngo. "My son's gone crazy and is now missing, and my daughter trembles with pain all the time." He pointed at Thuy laying on the bed shuddering. "My deformed grandson seems half-dead, and I myself have been stricken with disease. But if I sue the Americans for the sufferings of my family, I would get them into trouble and they would hate us, which would multiply the animosity between Americans and Vietnamese. The hatred from both sides is already too much for me." Mr. Ngo paused, searching for the right words. "The honorable thing to do was to fight and sacrifice myself for the peaceful life of our people today. The suffering of my and my comrades' families is the price we've paid for our country's peace. These are my deeply felt words. Our suffering makes sense this way, doesn't it?"

Pham Hoang listened to Mr. Ngo's sincere words with amazement, impressed by Mr. Ngo's generous and tolerant heart. He said,

"You are a great soldier who has sacrificed himself for the benefit of our people. But it's very hard for your family, I know, because the government can only provide you with just a small pension, and the Commune itself is too poor to help. I am very sorry for that."

As Pham Hoang left, Mr. Ngo stood up to say good-bye. Then he slowly groped his way to the ancestral altar, opened the tin box atop the altar and removed his letter to the American chemical company. He took a few sticks of incense and a box of matches and, feeling his way along the wall, slowly shuffled out to the yard and sat on the ground. After a while, he struck a match and lit the incense, then set the letter of complaint on fire too. The letter burst into flame and spread its heat to his face. Though he could not see the flame, he must have felt that it burnt very fast. Meanwhile, the wind blew the ashes and smoke high into the sky.

Elmo Jumwalt,* an American river patrol boat captain who went to war in the south of Vietnam, had sprayed toxic chemicals along many rivers. At the time, he believed he was fulfilling his mission to clear the forest, making it possible to discover the VC and to protect American troops. After returning to the U.S., Jumwalt began to have nightmares in which ghosts with deformed bodies chased him everywhere. These nightmares repeated for many years. Sometimes the ghosts cried hysterically, knocked him down, and seized him, demanding that he help the toxic chemicals' victims.

After learning how the spraying of toxic chemicals had brought serious illnesses to many Vietnamese and their children, he realized his nightmares of deformed bodies were in a way true.

One spring, Jumwalt and his wife came to Vietnam to develop a project to support Agent Orange victims. He came to Ho Chi

*Minh Chuyen changed the name here slightly to indicate that he is fictionalizing the story of Elmo Zumwalt III.

Minh City for a few days, then visited some of the centers for Agent Orange victims in the north. The Nam Dinh provincial Association of Agent Orange Victims introduced him to Mr. Ngo's family. Though Jumwalt and his wife had heard Mr. Ngo's pitiful story, they still could not believe their eyes when they saw how hard they struggled for their living. Jumwalt appeared uneasy as Mr. Ngo's relatives and neighbors gathered around him. He must have worried they might rush upon him, beat him, or tear his body apart, because he and his wife stood near the door. But nothing happened to them. In fact, during the visit, none of Mr. Ngo's houseguests showed hatred toward them. Even when telling them their family's story, Mr. Ngo and Mrs. Cam conducted themselves graciously, demonstrating their generosity and tolerance.

Of course, Mr. Ngo could not see Jumwalt, a man who had actually sprayed Agent Orange. Mr. Ngo blinked his blind eyes and said, "If I had met you thirty years ago, I would not have hesitated to shoot you. But now, don't be afraid! I won't harm you." After a moment's pause, he continued. "I could not stop the suffering of my family and tens of thousands of other families by killing you. I can only wish that when you return to America, that you will tell the American people that we willingly forgive those who have caused this disaster for so many in Vietnam. But America should be responsible for the consequences of this crime and for the plight of the people it has affected."

After the translator delivered Mr. Ngo's speech, Jumwalt looked happy and relieved. "Thank you, and thank you to Vietnam," he said. "I will tell my country what you have said in all sincerity. As a small gesture of reconciliation, I would like to take your daughter to America for medical treatment. We believe our doctors can help cure the sores on her body. Please, don't worry, I will take full responsibility for her trip to the U.S. and for her medical treatment."

Thanks to Jumwalt's enthusiasm and sincere heart, as well as the support of the local authorities, three months later, Mr. Ngo's family bid Thuy farewell as she left for the U.S.

The last time I visited their house, Mr. Ngo lay on the floor not caring what happened around him. Mrs. Cam came to say hello and served me a cup of tea. I told her I was sorry to hear her family's bad news had not yet ended.

Mrs. Cam told me that Mr. Ngo had gotten worse. He began to have trouble breathing and felt pain in all parts of his body. He complained of feeling as though a very hot stream ran through his whole body. His skin began to fissure, splitting open and bleeding.

In occasional moments of lucidity, he told Mrs. Cam what he felt and saw in his delirium. She described one of his dreams, in which he was a healthy and energetic soldier who carried a pack on his back and a gun on his shoulder, going to war with his troops. But then he noticed the troops all had deformed bodies with very small legs and big, elongated heads. Frightened terribly, he retreated from the formation. But the deformed soldiers immediately rushed toward him and lifted him up in triumph, then let him loose to float above the ground on pink and yellow clouds. Suddenly the clouds turned orange and took him high into the blue sky.

"Many things appear to be worse," Mrs. Cam groaned. "But I want to show you one thing that will surprise you. Just a moment . . ." She stepped into the kitchen and called her daughter. "Thuy! Come say hello to our honored guest."

Thuy entered the living room and gave me a nod. I could scarcely recognize her. Her black, hairy face and hairy upper body had been replaced with smooth, white skin. With her fine new complexion, her brilliant eyes and shining hair made her a pretty girl.

"What a wonderful change!" I exclaimed. "You're a pretty girl now, do you know that?"

Mrs. Cam smiled. "She's been to America for medical treatment and just came back last month. You're a reporter; you should announce this news in the press."

"Isn't it wonderful!" Thuy exclaimed, looking at me. "The American doctors treated me very well. Living with Mr. and Mrs. Jumwalt made me very happy."

"And you're in good health now. Can I say that?"

"No, no, never!" Thuy said, rolling up her trousers to show me her hairy legs. "And I still have pain in my body."

Mrs. Cam shook her head and said: "Thanks to the Jumwalts' kindness, Thuy has a better complexion, but they could not cure her body." Mrs. Cam rolled up Thuy's shirt and pointed to the lesions scattered on Thuy's belly. "They hurt her all the time and the medicine doesn't work much. I have to help her to wash the sores with alcohol twice a day."

I was moved to pity by Thuy's suffering and Mrs. Cam's hard work.

"Mrs. Cam, I know you are working very hard," I said. "You are the only one taking care of the family."

"I don't know how to manage," Mrs. Cam said, weeping.

"I imagine Mr. Ngo's blindness would cause you a lot of trouble."

"Now he's not just blind, but completely crazy."

"What happened?"

"He started by going to the cemetery to weep for our eldest son. Night after night, he groped his way there, some strange instinct of the blind guiding him along the winding road. When he arrived he wept for our children, both living and dead. The wind carried his heartrending cry to the hamlet, where everyone could hear it.

"One night during a heavy rainstorm, Mr. Ngo went to the cemetery with a hoe on his shoulder. As usual, his instinct guided him past hundreds of tombs right to that of our eldest son. This night, he did not weep. Again and again, he chopped into the soil, soaked through by the heavy rain. After working a long time, he finally broke through the lid of the coffin. He took the remains of our son, wrapped them in his wet shirt, and carried them to our kitchen, where he burned them on a fire of rice husks.

"It was well after midnight when Ngo came to the side of the bed.

"'Cam! Get up,' he said. 'I've brought home Nhan's remains.'

"I got out of bed and Ngo led me by the hand to the kitchen. He pointed to the ashes.

"'These are the bones of our eldest son,' he told me.

"I was so frightened. There on the floor were the bones and skull of my child. I started shouting for the neighbors, 'Help! My husband's gone crazy! Help me!'

"The neighbors came to see what was the matter, and I showed them the bones in the kitchen, weeping. 'Look at the bones,' I said. 'Ngo dug up my son and burned his remains.'

"My neighbor, Mr. Duy, asked him why he dug up Nhan.

"'Why?' Ngo shouted, laughing. 'Because he ran away; I had to take him back.' Then Ngo held the blackened skull to his chest, saying, 'My son, my son, now you have returned. We've missed you so much.'"

Mrs. Cam began to weep. Between sobs, she asked me to arrange to take Mr. Ngo to a psychiatric hospital.

Before leaving, I promised to help her as soon as possible. I wanted to say something else to comfort her, but I couldn't. In this case, I think, words would make no sense.

Hanoi, 2005

TRANSLATED BY HUY LIEN AND CHARLES WAUGH

VO THI HAO

THE BLOOD OF LEAVES

"I'm going to die. You know? I'm falling apart . . ."

His pinched voice sounded like it came from hell. Surprised, I looked around, but there was only me and Huan in the bar. We sat on the low stools toward the back, near the rattan wall. He looked at me through a glass of coffee, one of the green ferns that hung from every rafter in the ceiling swaying above him.

I laughed. "Someone like you could live through a mortar attack."

My words dissolved into silence, unable to penetrate his blank stare. Huan handed me the biopsy report he'd just received from Hospital K.

Cancer.

Many people I knew had died from it already. A pulse of nausea rose in my throat each time I remembered the knots of green worms writhing in death from Agent Orange. Faced with such human cruelty, each of us was just like those worms.

Huan still had his looks. At forty-two, the light skin of his face still shone, framed by his neat sideburns. His large almond eyes looked as if he understood everything. Huan was a physician. He hadn't married yet, and now because of gastric cancer he never would.

I didn't dare look at him. Instead I fixed my gaze on the yellow leaves of the cycad suffering in its pot next to the bar. It was struggling to grow one small shoot. I angrily cursed the hospital's inability to cure my friend, but Huan suddenly changed the tone of his voice as if he didn't give a damn.

"I didn't invite you here to listen to me cry. The last few months, I've been trying to live with death, and finally, it's made everything clear. You know what a kid does when he's afraid of ghosts? First, he closes his eyes, and then he shouts. When he tires from shouting, he peeks open one eye. Then he blinks. At last, he opens his eyes wide. That's what I've done, and now my panic is over. Dying like this isn't so bad. The sooner I go, the more people will pity me. You'll come to the funeral, right?" Huan smiled bitterly.

I looked away and wiped the tears from my eyeglasses. Huan's coffin would be sealed with the sharp taps of a hammer.

The bar girl appeared from the back wearing a ridiculous miniskirt that forced her to walk with tiny, mincing steps. She stood next to Huan and cocked her hip. From his seat on the low stool, his forehead came right up to the top of her thigh.

"Want anything else, Sugar?"

I glared at her, thinking of throwing the ashtray at her brazen face. I must've looked crazy.

She walked away immediately, dismissing us over her shoulder: "Fuck off! Guys like you are all talk, no money. Posers!"

Huan chuckled like a guy who'd just crossed a river and then gazed back with appreciation for the decrepit ferry. She was right. In the near future, he would be completely broke. Not even dirty words could stir up the coming dark.

Suddenly, Huan said, "Hey, I called you here for something else." Then he whispered, "There! Look!"

Instantly, the wounded panther look disappeared from his face. His eyelashes quivered like those of a guy falling in love.

I looked where he pointed, expecting to see the shadow of a charming girl at the top of the street. At first there was only a speck, then a very small girl appeared, just about one meter in height. She had a flat chest and wide open eyes.

Her mouth had a white scar like from cleft-lip surgery, pulling it to the right. Unlike the upper lip, the lower one was full and red like the petal of a flower, with a hollow below it like a small dimpled cheek. She held an old basket like those made in the sixties. Her limp made her look like a flower picker selling on the street. She walked so slowly I couldn't help but get a good look at her, even though I was trying to see up the sidewalk past her. The girl Huan was waiting for had to be a beauty.

"What are you looking for? Listen!"

From his pocket, Huan withdrew a very thick letter, covered by a pink layer of nylon and scented with perfume.

"Just read—then you'll know."

On the envelope, someone had written, "To Mr. M," in irregular handwriting. Maybe the letter belonged to a daydreamer.

I asked Huan, "Are you secretly reading someone else's mail?"

"It's mine," he said flatly. "A love letter. Just read it."

Blue beads on the paper looked like tears.

My Love!

It has been four months since I received your last letter. I feel like dying. My sister Van told me that missing a letter is normal. I have begun to think you have already dissolved like smoke.

Dear You! The Creator must have been in his cups while making me. When I was fourteen, I resolved to kill myself by drinking a bowl of oleander water. Father told me I stuffed my head with too many novels. And that I am a work of shame. From then on, I always tried to be absent when guests visited my house. That should have pleased him.

I earned good marks at school, high enough to enter university, but no university wanted such an ugly student. I used to wish I was crazy because the crazy ones are always happy living and floating in their miraculous world without ever realizing who they are. I burned incense often and prayed for an end to my life. How did God have the heart to put a good brain inside the head of someone like me, a girl he made by drunken mistake?

Instead of going to university, I stayed at home and got acquainted with pots and pans, cats and novels. My first lover was Mr. Rochester, the character from *Jane Eyre*. Every night, I felt Mr. Rochester was looking and smiling at me. He would open his dark coat and pull me inside, hold me close to his chest. Then we both went out.

When I realized he was so tall, so much more than just little me, I felt ashamed. I retracted my head into the coat. But Mr. Rochester could see my feelings. He stopped and said, 'Hey, my dear, ugly girl! You would like me to be smaller, wouldn't you?'

I nodded my head gratefully, craning my neck around to look at him. Out of the blue, jet planes came and screamed. Houses collapsed. Children cried.

Mr. Rochester set me down and rushed into a flaming building. After several minutes of horrible waiting, people carried him out on a stretcher. Rochester was dead. His eyes had turned into two red holes.

Even in my dreams, God won't let me feel easy. He did not give me the right to enjoy a true, full dream.

When I cried about such things, my brother Tuan would stroke my hair quietly. It didn't take long for all the little kid games he consoled me with when we were children to pass into uselessness.

All the more reason I treasure your letters!

Sometimes I wonder whether you are really real, or just a dream like Rochester. Why do you have to hide from me? I want to see you. If I do, then I'll know you're real. But I'm also frightened that if I find you there will be no more letters, so I'm trying to be content with letters alone. For the last three years, I've carried your first letter in a small silk pouch beneath my undershirt.

I have to lie to myself all the time to avoid thinking that a day will come when I will have neither a letter nor you. When that day comes, I will die.

I already know what death will feel like. I learned when I received notification of Tuan's death, my dear brother, who loved me most in this life. There was no letter from you for such a long time. I felt like dying myself. The shock of Tuan's death gave my mother a kind of stroke. The whole day, her eyes bobbed wildly all over the room, looking at me and laughing as if I were a stranger. My father also fell ill. His high blood pressure gave him intense headaches and blurred his vision. I have to lead him around the house now. And my poor sister, she's still grieving for Tuan, and at the same time she just found out her husband has cheated on her.

I've come to the conclusion that it's hard for good people to meet good luck.

That's why I worry for you too.

God must have read my thoughts and understood my need. When you recovered from your illness and your letters began to arrive again, I could live again, even though I worried that your weakened condition had made your writing a little strange.

But the world is full of strange and mysterious things. And the most mysterious thing is you.

My Dear! I will be on this earth as long as your letters still come to me . . .

The letter was as long as a novel, but it was so crazy it drew me in. More than just the words on the page, it almost seemed mystical somehow. When I ran my fingers over the words, in my mind a white cathedral appeared. Inside, the cathedral echoed with the beating of a tiny heart.

"That's her letter," I said, pointing to where the girl had passed.

"Yes."

"You mean . . . you love her?"

"No. It's not like that. I'm not blind."

"So . . . ?"

"You can guess I wrote those letters, right? But that's just part of the story."

He leaned back, caressed the stunted cycad's leaf and curved it like a golden comb. Then he told me a story, the unbelievable kind you only read about in books.

"Even though several years have passed," he said, "whenever I think about it, I still feel anxious, like something's rushing in my heart.

"In '74, I fought in the area around Ban Me Thuot with a young painter named Tuan. He'd joined the army the year before me and was the kind of guy to speak just a few words the whole day. His eyes were always really sad. Every night, beneath his blanket, Tuan wrote letters by flashlight. The faint glow of his blanket always creeped out the guys in the unit because it looked like those low, ghostly flames that rise up from the swamps. Everybody said he must be writing beautiful letters to his beautiful girlfriend in Hanoi, trying to use honeyed words to keep from losing her. You were a soldier, so you know, right? During the war, people attached their hearts to others to protect themselves. It kept them from falling apart at the sight of every horrible thing. So even though Tuan proved himself on the battlefield, our sergeant reported all the letter writing as a weakness, and Tuan had to be observed for signs of desertion.

"One gloomy afternoon in April, he and I were assigned to the same position at the far end of the skirmish line. We'd already won the battle, but as we chased the enemy over the ridge, both sides kept tabs on each other, popping off occasional shots. Still a greenhorn, I felt overwhelmed by the fighting in the jungle and had fallen behind. Tuan dropped back, waiting for me. No longer alone, I felt safe enough to plop down to the ground.

"'I'm so thirsty,' I croaked. I was almost out of breath.

"Tuan stopped walking. The earth all around had turned blackish brown. The trees had completely lost their foliage, leaving the black branches wavering and clutching at everything like ghosts. Tuan stooped down and began to root through the dead leaves and soil. After a minute, he showed me what he'd been looking for: a small, dirty thing shaped like a big toe. He gave it to me and said, 'Break it open, and suck on it. It'll make you less thirsty.'

"Even though my throat felt scorched, I looked at the thing with disgust. Tuan took it back and tore it in half. In his palm, the two halves began to squirm. A snail.

"'Maybe the only living thing left in the forest,' he said. 'How lucky! Here, hold it in your mouth a few seconds if you can, then swallow it.'

"The idea of it made me gag. But finally, so thirsty, I put the snail on my tongue. I swallowed it down and covered my mouth. Tears rolled down my face. Immediately, alongside the queasiness, a cool sensation spread over my tongue. I was conscious again. Opening my eyes, I saw Tuan's Adam's apple bobbing up and down. He was even thirstier than me.

"'Ho Chi Minh Trail ginseng,' he said, grinning. 'It's not too terrible.'

"I grimaced at him. Then we both burst out laughing, Tuan's face lighting up like a kid's. He found a small green egg at his feet, picked it up and tossed it to me.

"'It's a snake egg,' he said. 'When I was young, my little sister Tam and I had such a close call. We incubated an egg we'd found at the botanical garden. Tam thought it was magic. When it hatched, instead of the phoenix we thought we had, out came a snake.'

"Suddenly, there was a 'Pop!' and Tuan placed his hand over his chest. Saying nothing, he sank lower and lower. Finally he bent down. The back of his hand slowly disappeared beneath a red wash of blood. The forest went silent.

"Frightened, I shouted and started running. After several steps, I stumbled and fell into the dried up remains of a bush. Regaining sense, I ran back breathlessly. Cradling Tuan's head in one arm, I shouted at him, trying to wake him up.

"Tuan opened his eyes. A spasm of pain sent tears rolling into his hair.

"I wrapped a bandage around his chest, but in just a moment the blood soaked all the way through. The bullet had gone in under his collarbone but didn't come out the other side. I didn't know what to do except lay him in my lap, patting his chest. His blood soaked through his clothes into mine. Soon I was sitting in a puddle of it. I felt like it was my blood too.

"Tuan didn't spend his last words on his own pain. Instead, he told me about his sister, Tam. All the letters under the swamp fire light had been for her.

"'If I die,' he said, 'there will be no letter, and she will die also. I was the one who took the bowl of oleander water from her hands. I have sent her the love letters.'

"I couldn't believe it.

"He told me, 'She believes because she wants to. She has stuffed her head with a lot of absurd things . . . but she needs love as much as she needs to drink water.'

"Tuan's eyes went blank. He curled up, clawing a handful of earth and putting it into his mouth. The gravel cracked between his clenched teeth. He turned his head toward me, about to speak, to ask something. Then it rolled back, his eyes wide, his face white as gypsum.

"I screamed and threw myself on the ground like a child. Alone in the jungle, with his body on top of me, I felt like the dead black trees would crash down on me at any second. As night fell, a mist settled between us, the trees, and the stars.

"When I calmed down, I began to dig with my bayonet. Thoroughly exhausted, I managed to scratch out a shallow pit and mound the soil over my friend. I spent the rest of the night by the grave. By then, no fear lingered in my mind. I mulled over silly philosophical questions about life's sorrow. In the morning, when I dragged myself back into camp carrying two packs and two guns, everyone shouted for the medic to bandage me up because the blood smeared all over me smelled like death.

"A week later, I opened Tuan's bag and found his last letter, the one he hadn't yet sent. I rewrote it again and again to imitate his handwriting and to learn by heart his romantic writing style. After several months of practice, I finally sent the letter to Tam. Tuan had addressed the envelope to Nguyen Thi Tam and placed it inside another envelope addressed to Ms. Thanh Van, 47 Hang Chuoi Street, Ha Noi. I guessed Ms. Thanh Van might be the postwoman, in on Tuan's secret.

"Copying Tuan's handwriting took practice, but it was a lot easier than coming up with my own material. Before, I thought doing something like this only happened in novels. I never expected to find myself a character in such a plot. In fact, I'd been too lazy to write any letters at all before this, not even to my own parents, but with the image of Tuan's dying eyes driving me, I really had to work at it. And by writing I began to love life more than ever.

"I wrote my eleventh letter at the end of the war. I came home to Hanoi and visited Tuan's family to give them his belongings. When I saw Tam, I wondered how the Creator could make such a girl think and dream like others.

"At some point, I became two people. In one life, I was the character in a romantic novel who played an anonymous guy struggling to collect fragments of a story about a dreaming, unreachable love into a letter to a girl without hope. In the other, I actually began to love Tam. Her face veiled by a sheer white veil, she loomed near and far. Flickering in my imagination, her eyes shone with tears, and her pink lips trembled. She was like mist, like honey, like the Virgin Mary.

"So, I embraced an unreal love of my own. As someone who sowed illusion for others, now I reaped an illusion for myself. Work swept away everything. Graduate school, my dissertation, conferences . . . I had no idea how time was passing. And I might have been able to marry a nice woman if I did not always feel the illusion beside me, making every other woman seem common."

Huan ran his fingers through his hair, catching a white one between his two fingers. Tears came to his eyes.

"Now, I'm going to die. Like Tuan, I'm about to die too young. If I'm luckier than him, it's only because I've had enough time to find someone to replace me. A person kind enough to keep up such an awkward job. Someone who can write and someone just a little bit crazy."

"Me? I have a wife!"

"Don't try to argue! Your were a soldier too. Living through war made us strange. We don't really fit into the world today. Maybe that's unnatural and unbelievable, but it's true. And that's the most telling part of the sad stories the next generation might tell about the war."

"But . . ."

"Stop. It's the last request of a dying man."

Then, lonely Huan stood up and would not allow me to say good-bye.

That night, the whole war came back in my dreams. The entire nation clamored into battle. Everyone wore rubber sandals, held guns, and carried letters close to their chests. Pages from stories about letters flew through the air with misplaced and misdirected letters falling like leaves. I could see myself clearly in that scene, skin sallow, running, holding a letter, shouting "Attack!" before diving to the earth.

In the days that followed, Huan withered like a tree. When I visited, he often lay on the bed, writhing and coughing up blood. When he felt better, he read Tam's letters again and again.

On a beautiful, sunny day, a day no one thought of death, Huan passed away. I came into his room, where he lay on his bed as if sleeping. He had left me a note:

"When we were students, we used to enjoy 'The last leaf' story together. Do you know the meaning of 'the last leaf' to a person about to die? I don't have that leaf. Please lay the last leaf on Tam's doorstep. Good-bye."

I felt woozy. I waved down a cyclo to announce Huan's death.

The street bubbled with hostility. A crowd had gathered at an intersection. Someone shouted: "A robber just snatched gold earrings from that woman in the white shirt." The woman's shoulders were covered in blood. War's not the only place to find it.

At the front gate of the courthouse, an old man had just lost his case to keep his house from being demolished. Sitting on the curb, holding his face, he said: "Justice! Help me! Where is justice?" Not far from the old man, a ruddy-faced businessman averted his gaze from a beggar as he got into his black Mercedes and sped away.

Huan's hearse would soon pass through this crowd, among the raving people and worldly suffering.

I did not see Tam at the funeral. After the last mourner had gone, I turned my head round and thought for a second I saw a tiny flower picker behind a gravestone wafting incense. It might have been a mirage.

It was my turn to secretly write a letter to Tam. Sinking behind a messy pile of papers at my office, I wrote a letter to Tam, the whole time afraid of being caught. I also began going some afternoons to the café with the cycads to sit alone and watch Tam move slowly up the street.

I already had a wife whom I loved dearly. So it was not easy for me to compose these letters. My work conveyed little sense of a living soul.

Sometimes, I was so busy or lazy it took weeks to finish a letter. At night, with my wife in my arms, I would fall asleep imagining four eyes hanging in the air. They looked like leaves. Two of the four leaves winked and looked at me. The other two leaves sagged. Blood gradually covered them drop by drop. Then I'd wake up, holding my pounding heart.

My wife turned suspicious. She began to think I was having an affair with another woman. More and more frequently, little things set her off.

Depressed, I increasingly went to the café.

One day, and then for several afternoons after, I did not see Tam. At the end of the week, I went to the address on Hang Chuoi and asked the postwoman where to find her.

At Tam's house, her father limped around like a ghost. She lay on a bed near the window on the first floor. Tiny blood vessels criss-crossed her pale cheeks.

I tried to saunter by. But she saw me, held her head up and said, "I know you're the one sending the letters to me. The writing style has changed twice now. You are Hoang. I've seen you sitting in the Huong Dem café watching me. When the handwriting seemed strange, I asked the mail carrier and I knew . . ."

Tam's eyes welled with tears, but she did not cry.

"Over the years, you three have been a dry hand extended to a drowning girl. But when Huan died, the little Mr. Rochester-loving girl also died. The days when I lied to myself, pretending a magic creature from inside an egg would rescue me have gone. It's time I became a woman, even if it's hard for me to bear."

When I tried to stop Tam, she put up a finger:

"Don't worry. I won't die. How could I destroy all your hard work? Just don't write anything to me, okay? Instead, visit once in a while. Your world is endless but mine is tiny. I have to return to that world.

"On the horizon, there might be a man, tiny like me. And if he were to exist, he would belong to me. He would come, smile a big, wide smile, and say, 'Hey, Little Miss Ugly, have you been waiting long for me?'"

I left the house wearing sunglasses to avoid anyone seeing my red eyes.

I went to Huan's grave, remembering the song he used to sing:

Go to sleep little one, tired of all your troubles.
Go to sleep little one, return to the middle of your dream.
Go to sleep little one, go to sleep—you've suffered enough . . .

Over his grave, the flickering wind blew through a patch of forget-me-nots, singing:

Sleep. . . .

Hanoi, 2005
TRANSLATED BY LENA LE AND CHARLES WAUGH

THU TRAN

THE QUIET POPLAR

Any time the stress of the office got to be too much, Bich Tra would turn to her window on the eighth floor to gaze down at the city below. Whether mist enshrouded dawn or late afternoon sun, she always found something within her view to impress her; the streets, trees, and river reminding her of beautiful paintings. Each set of roofs became in her imagination another still life, the painted backdrop to the tumbled lives of the big city's working class. It seemed each roof had its own level and building material. In the east, a square roof made of a dark purple, imitation corrugated steel sparkled under morning sunlight. At a lower level, uneven roofs made of real corrugated steel had over their long lives already turned a rusty brown. Most of the roofs closer to her office had been tiled in various colors, using a wide variety of styles: double tile, hook tile, even imitation tile made from plastic. But as much pleasure as she obtained from her view, it always seemed to her the "still lives" lacked something, like the white hand-kerchief laid across a flower vase she'd seen in a painting at a gallery in the old district. Or the blade of grass that managed to seem to waver in the *Carrots and Potatoes* painting hung on her living room wall. Each time at the window, she looked for something new.

"How could I have missed that?" she wondered one day, seeing a low, charcoal gray roof for the first time. It crouched over its small cottage toward a lone green poplar, just downwind from a factory's twin chimneys. When she mentioned the green poplar to her friend, Mai Linh, whose desk was next to hers, Mai Linh craned her neck toward the window and asked, "Which one do you mean?"

"That one," said Bich Tra. She walked to the window and pointed to an area near the horizon. "It's the only tree in that bit of land below the old airport."

Mai Linh shrugged her shoulders and said, "Girl, that's no poplar. It's a willow. I think poplars only grow in Russia."

Momentarily struck dumb by Mai Linh's assertion, Bich Tra knew at once she'd gotten the name wrong, but she tried to save face: "It doesn't matter if we call it a poplar; they're both in the same family."

Bich Tra knew why she liked thinking of the tree as a poplar. Her favorite book was a translated collection of Chingiz Aitmatov's stories called *The Little Poplar with a Red Scarf* that Quang had given to her on her twentieth birthday. In those days, she dearly loved all the Russian things he introduced to her. She loved smoked salmon. She loved the ballet. And she loved the poets like Akhmatova and Esenin who expressed such an intense nostalgia for the old Russia. A favorite Tchaikovsky song came flickering through her mind:

Again, as before, I'm alone,
Again I'm filled with longing.
A poplar stands by the window,
Flooded with moonlight.

A poplar stands by the window,
The leaves are whispering about something.
The sky is aflame with stars . . .
Where, now, darling, are you?*

*Peter Ilich Tchaikovsky and Daniil Ratgauz, "Again, as before, Alone," Op. 73, No. 6, trans. Richard D. Sylvester, *Tchaikovsky's Complete Songs: A Companion with Texts and Translations* (Bloomington: Indiana University Press, 2002), 281–82.

Quang still lived far away in Russia. After many years of study, he finally gave up on his PhD dissertation and switched careers to make money as a businessman, returning to Viet Nam only to buy consumer goods for export to Russia. His Russian wife, Natasha, was as beautiful as a fashion model, but Quang still always called Bich Tra and arranged to meet with her. Many times she had resolved not to see him again, to try to forget the wound she'd been nursing for so long. But her heart had its own way of doing things, and so she continued to allow him to visit her several times each year.

Bich Tra watched her poplar attentively. Did it tremble? It seemed its long branches shook now and then. It had been the same at this hour the day before, and perhaps also the day before that. She adjusted her glasses to watch her favorite still life more carefully. If ever the poplar were to be cut down, her painting would be ruined; no white handkerchief lying across the flower vase, no blade of grass wavering over the carrots and potatoes. . . . The poplar really was shaking.

Bich Tra went to Mai Linh and asked, "Do you know the way to the cottage with the poplar?"

"Just take the elevator to the ground floor," said Mai Linh, raising her face and smiling, "then you'll find it somewhere outside."

"Stop kidding!" complained Bich Tra.

"It looks pretty close as the crow flies," said Mai Linh, knocking her fingers on the table, "but I bet it's not so easy to get to. They call it the runway hamlet."

It was not so difficult to find the house by the willow after all. The house had almost no furnishings but had been kept very clean.

A fourteen- or fifteen-year-old girl with sparkling eyes who crept stealthily like a little cat met Bich Tra at the door and quietly invited her inside: "Please sit down, and I will call my father."

"No! No, thank you, there's no need to call him," said Bich Tra, hurriedly. "I just want to ask you something."

The girl clasped her hands together politely. "What can I do for you?"

Bich Tra struggled to think what to say to the girl. Of course she couldn't ask her directly about the shaking tree because the question would seem so odd and silly. How could a young girl understand the complicated and nostalgic feelings of love and loss that the tree had evoked in her? Even her own mother didn't understand. Her mother thought Bich Tra had suffered some kind of nervous breakdown and should check into the hospital for treatment. Only old people liked to think so much about the past. Bich Tra had begun to wonder whether, at forty, her nostalgia was a sign her youth had finally run out. Regardless, as she had grown into womanhood, the little poplar with a red scarf had also grown in her heart. She could never let it go.

While the little girl stared at her expectantly, Bich Tra finally came up with a lie: "I want to buy a house in the neighborhood here. I thought maybe you could tell me something about it."

"You want to buy a house in this area?" the girl gasped. "Please, Miss, don't even think about it. In the past year, just about everyone has been trying to get away. Everyone's afraid of the K."

"What do you mean, 'the K'?"

"Sorry, Miss, I thought everyone knew K means cancer. Five people from our hamlet have died from it this year. During the war, the airbase soil and water were contaminated. Mrs. Vien, one of my teachers, told my class that Agent Orange killed the trees and made people's hair fall out. She said she remembers when she was a child, sometimes the American planes also sprayed chemicals over her neighborhood. The old men called the spray American piss because it smelled so nasty. Agent Orange causes all kinds of incurable diseases, but cancer is the worst. That's what my father has too. Here, I'll show you something."

The naive girl led Bich Tra by the hand to the willow in the yard. She pointed at the deep cuts lining the willow's trunk: "Each time Daddy's pain gets too hard to bear, he chops at the trunk with a cleaver. The deeper the cut, the worse his pains. For some reason it seems to help him feel better."

With a sting in her heart, Bich Tra asked, "How do you know your daddy cuts deeper when he feels more pain?"

"I'm guessing that's the way it is. I've read in the newspaper about an invention that lets people experience what a patient feels, but since I don't have one of them, I have to look at the cuts on the trunk to guess what Daddy feels."

Bich Tra liked the girl. She seemed very smart and energetic. Her name was Thanh Thao, and she was in the ninth grade. She said she only got medium-level marks and was not an excellent student because she had been taking care of her father all by herself since her mother left them. When her mother found out that it was cancer that had caused her father's suffering, she so feared for their six-year-old boy's health that she fled with him in the middle of the night. All that was left of her in the morning was a note.

"Where is your daddy now?" asked Bich Tra.

"He never leaves the house," said Thao. "At least he doesn't go far. There's a little hut down by the spinach pond where he goes to work on his painting. He doesn't paint for money any more, just to ease his sadness and pain."

Thanh Thao explained that her father, Phong, did not consider himself much of a painter, but he was a very skilled draftsman.

Everything he drew came out true to life and beautiful. But after his customers learned he had cancer, no one came to place orders for drawings or paintings, assuming he probably wouldn't finish the job. That was another reason her mother gave for leaving.

Thao smacked her lips, looked outside, and said, "My mother promised she would make some money to support Daddy and me. But I know she'll never come home again. The day before she left, she argued with Daddy about Nheo, my brother, saying because of his illness he couldn't support him any more. I missed my mother when she left, but I could never desert my father. We are poor, and our life is hard, but we can survive. The school helps by giving me my textbooks and school supplies. Each month we get about two hundred dong from my mother and some money from the Agent Orange victims' fund. Daddy gets a pension from them even though he hasn't had a test to prove his cancer came from Agent Orange. The only tests for that are in America and cost thousands of dollars. But some foreign scientists studied the water and soil and vegetables here and found really high levels of dioxin, so Daddy and some disabled kids in the neighborhood get a little money each month, and sometimes gifts from charities."

Bich Tra was moved by the little girl's plain-spoken and deeply felt words and loved the gray cottage and little poplar all the more. She began to think of doing something for the poor man and his daughter.

Thanh Thao took Bich Tra to the hut above the spinach pond. A man with a sickly yellow complexion sat inside, leaning against the hut's central column. His eyes were closed in sleep, or maybe meditation.

As they crossed the shaky wooden bridge, Thanh Thao called, "Daddy! I've just made friends with this lady. She's really nice and sweet. Open your eyes, please!"

Phong's eyes remained shut, as if he hadn't heard. His pain had put him into a trance.

Thao pointed to the paintings scattered on the floor along the walls of the hut. "These are imitations of famous paintings. Once when we didn't have money for food, he tried to sell them, but no one wanted them."

Not wanting to interrupt Phong's meditation, Bich Tra asked Thao to bring her some of the best of those paintings. After looking through them, she chose two and gave the little girl some money.

Thao led Bich Tra by the hand to the door and said, "Good-bye. Please come see us again." As Bich Tra rode away, the girl waved her hand affectionately, calling, "Don't forget the house with the green willow!"

Phong strummed a guitar, singing:

I'll love you tenderly, even in a dream
The love from my heart is like the gentlest wind
Whispering down a mountain stream.

Thanh Thao had never been so happy. She was busy preparing dinner for the three of them. Bich Tra helped her make the spring rolls, which were as small as her little finger.

"It's so strange to make such a little roll," Bich Tra teased. "We'll have to eat them like tigers gulping down tiny candies."

Thao laughed and said, "Daddy likes the ones that are really tiny and crisp. He used to eat the regular size spring rolls one teeny bite at a time."

Phong looked at the two of them, nodded his head, and sang louder and more passionately. The little cottage by the "poplar" had never been so merry and warm.

After dinner, Bich Tra selected several of Phong's paintings for clients who had seen the works she'd bought for herself, plus she revealed that she had taken orders for others. A lady she knew who owned a clock shop wanted a painting of a cat with a red collar as a birthday present for her grandson. An English teacher who lived in her neighborhood asked her to request a medium sized landscape similar to Levitan's *Golden Autumn* for his classroom. And a coffee shop owner wanted a portrait of the famous songwriter Trinh Cong Son inspired by her favorite song, "Dreamland."

Over the next six months, the orders Bich Tra brought to Phong allowed him to earn a small income, just enough to survive, but also enough to let Phong begin to believe again in the significance of his life and to let the little family find some happiness. This was the most important thing.

One day, after accepting Phong's invitation to sit and have some tea, Bich Tra gazed at him attentively.

"Why do you look at me like that?" he asked.

She answered with concern in her voice. "You look very pale lately. Have you been taking your medicine?"

"Of course. It's important because you're the one who bought the medicine. When I take this snake-bone powder, at first I feel like my guts are on fire, but then somehow my pain eases away. It seems like my stomach cells have finally decided to call off the strike and come back to work."

She laughed with him. Opening her bag, she placed several vials on the table. "I brought a whole month's supply of medicine this time instead of a week's. My office is sending me to Hanoi for a four-week training program. I'll be back by the time you need more. And here's a stack of orders for more paintings, plus an advance for fifty percent of the total. They'll pay the rest when you finish."

"I worry you're spending too much time taking all these orders," said Phong. "I don't want to get you into trouble with these tri-fling things. Maybe it would be better to have Thanh Thao deliver the paintings? You need time to develop your own business con-tracts."

Bich Tra ignored him. "You've made good progress with your paint-ings lately. You might even win a prize one day. Who knows?"

"If so, maybe you can arrange an exhibition of my work after I die," said Phong, smiling mischievously. "In the center of the room full of my paintings, you can make a display out of my spoiled stomach in a glass jar."

Bich Tra laughed reluctantly this time, fighting back a tear and the pain in her heart. She wished that when Phong felt some relief from his pain and seemed to be very happy he could forget about his illness, even if just for a moment. She tried to change the subject: "Tell the truth—does the snake-bone powder really work?"

"It does!" he laughed. He pointed at the yard. "Look, no new cuts on our poplar!"

Bich Tra smiled and nodded her head. It was a great pleasure to hear Phong call the willow tree a poplar. It had become as dear to them as it was to her. It had become *"our* poplar."

She said, "I hope it keeps working so well. It's like they say, *The patient's good luck is more important than good medicine."*

With the orders and medicine taken care of, Bich Tra quickly made an excuse to leave. She didn't feel comfortable being alone with Phong, despite Thao's purposeful encouragement. Opening herself up to someone seemed impossible after her relationship with Quang had fallen apart so horribly; she just couldn't let herself have more bad luck. She insisted on treating Thao and her father as her very good friends, and to that end she had even made a schedule to visit only once every other week. But it hadn't lasted. She couldn't stop herself from seeing them more often. Once, she had visited every day for ten days, bringing immeasurable happiness to the little cottage. After returning home from her visits, she often thought about Phong, and came to realize his detachment from others was a mask that hid his real sympathy and affections. Her presence in the cottage gradually enabled him to reveal his true self. He worked harder on his paintings, endowing them with his love of life and hope for a better existence in a pure and healthy environment. She knew he would never be a famous artist, but his works moved her deeply because the scenes and portraits he painted were so close to her. Each time she came to the cottage, he had painted something new. Orchids in warm and deep shades of violet; a window frame suffused with light blue cooking smoke; a portrait of Thao that captured her round eyes full of hope; and Nheo, his son, smiling and flying a kite among pink and yellow clouds.

With her, he could finally express his passion for life. He liked to poeticize the most trivial aspects of daily life: the loud voice of the woman who bought and sold empty bottles on the street; sunshine sparkling through the vent in the roof; one lonely spinach flower on a pond full of water-spangles; field mice chasing one another in a corner of the hut. . . . Often now his face brightened with a cheerful smile.

In her apartment, the telephone was ringing. She glanced at the clock. At nearly one in the morning, it had to be Quang, calling from Russia.

She stood quietly, wrapped in his warm, passionate embrace.

"I have to leave," said Quang. "I'll be back next year."

She smiled sadly and nodded her head. She didn't speak, didn't ask him about the future. He could come and go as he pleased. It wasn't his fault she couldn't say good-bye to her own little poplar with a red scarf and the mythical Russia and passionate and hopeless love that went with it. But this time she didn't take Quang to the airport, and he didn't seem surprised. It was as if they both knew if he asked she would only answer that parting at the airport always made her sad, and Quang would agree, saying, "You're right, it's better for us this way." Quang's taxi pulled away from the curb, raising the dust. She coughed and pulled her collar higher on her neck. She had to get back to the office. During Quang's visit, she used up the last of her vacation days and even called in sick for two more. Before that, she'd been in the capital for a month, meaning all together she'd been away for five weeks. Many things at work and at home needed to be done.

When from her office window Bich Tra saw the little poplar shaking endlessly, it seemed her heart would break into pieces. She wrapped her arms around herself and turned back to find Mai Linh watching her.

"You should go out there right away," said Mai Linh. "Your poplar has been shaking all the time the past few days."

Bich Tra hurried to the elevator. In the parking lot, she was so anxious she couldn't find her motorbike. The watchman shook his head and said, "You look really upset. Maybe riding your motorbike isn't a good idea anyway. I'll call a taxi."

Running down the narrow alley leading to the cottage, she had to pause several times to catch her breath. She called out before she'd even reached the porch: "Thao! Thao!"

The little girl was kneeling beneath the "poplar." Her thin shoulders shook. She cradled her head in one arm, the cleaver grasped tightly in her other hand. Bich Tra rushed to her side, embracing her.

"What's wrong? Where's your daddy?"

The girl cried bitterly, "I shook the tree all the week, but you didn't come."

She helped Thao to her feet. Bich Tra took the cleaver and threw it into the dirt at the base of the "poplar." Sap as red as blood flowed from the tree's many new cuts.

Bich Tra's tears began to pour down her cheeks. She pursed her lips tightly to avoid weeping out loud.

A woman dressed in mourning clothes stood beside the family altar. Seeing Bich Tra, her expression turned suspicious and unpleasant. Bich Tra knew who she was. The six-year-old boy stood across the altar from her, looking at his father's picture.

Thao took Bich Tra's hand and sobbed out what had happened: "Mommy came home without telling us. And when she said she wanted to sell the small plot of land by the spinach pond to some people she knew, his face went white, and suddenly, he died."

So many unexpected things happen in this world to cause people to be sad and regretful. Phong unexpectedly died after the five weeks they had not seen each other. She had unexpectedly taken a week's leave to be with Quang, even though she'd tried not to, unable to resist her nostalgia for the "little poplar with a red scarf."

It was three in the morning, but Bich Tra could not sleep. Phong's image kept haunting her mind. She tried listening to one of her favorite CDs, but with every song she imagined him sitting next to her, listening to the sweet melody. His white teeth, shining in a relieved smile, brightened his face. She had to turn it off. Worse, his paintings sat propped against the walls all over her apartment, reminding her of his love and hope for a better life. In just over six months, he had finished hundreds of commissioned paintings.

Once, he had said, "You're great at marketing. All your customer-acquaintances have good taste."

"Yes," she answered, "my friends are people of taste."

She had brought snake-bone powder to treat his pain, even though she didn't really believe it had medicinal value. Even so, she believed he would survive. She had convinced herself that the old saying was true: *A person full of the love of life cannot disappear from the world.* In fact, she had no customers. She had used most of her income to buy all the paintings herself, believing her orders were the real medicine, feeding the spark of vitality that had survived in his ill body until it shone like the brightest beams of sunset. Moreover, they had brightened the little girl's face with happy smiles and given Bich Tra confidence that it was all right that the little poplar with a red scarf had grown entwined around her heart.

Lying on the bed, suddenly she felt a throbbing pain in her chest. She went to her medicine cabinet for an aspirin and found the packet of snake-bone powder Thao had returned to her that morning. Thao had told her that Phong had tried the same stuff several months before Bich Tra had first visited, but only for a short time, finding the high temperature it caused in his body unbearable.

"'We can't change our fate,'" she recalled him saying. "'I don't care about taking medicine.' But when you came to see us and brought him a lot of this same medicine, he took it all the time and the pain went away. Do you believe self-confidence can help people fight off the pain caused by illness? I think sometimes it can happen. Every time you came to see us, Daddy tried his best to control his pain so he didn't have to cut the trunk of 'our poplar.' While you were gone, he endured his pain by clenching his teeth and sitting by the easel to draw your portrait. He made it from memory, but it is the living image of you, don't you think?"

Bich Tra liked the portrait very much, even though it was unfinished. In it she appeared both strong and sweet, her lips indisposed to love.

Thao had told her that during Phong's last days the unbearable pain made it impossible for him to sit at the easel to finish the portrait.

Bich Tra leaned against the cabinet and raised her eyes to the picture of Phong hung on the wall next to the unfinished portrait. He was smiling, amused. A vase of white tuberoses sat on the cabinet, scenting the whole room with their sweet fragrance. She took her portrait from the wall, embraced it in her arms, and sank to the floor, petrified with sadness.

Dark, steamy clouds weighed down the sky. But the rain would not fall, and the air of the city began to swelter early in the morning. A church bell tolled mournfully. One more person just passed away.

Ho Chi Minh City, 2007
TRANSLATED BY CHARLES WAUGH AND HUY LIEN

LE CAO DAI AND THE

AGENT ORANGE SUFFERERS

A graduate of the Viet Nam Medical University operating in the jungle from 1947 to 1953 during the war of resistance against France, Le Cao Dai helped to establish Military Hospital 211 in the Central Highlands during the American War, serving as its first director from 1964 to 1969. He lived and worked in the A Sau and A Luoi areas of Thua Thien Hue Province for ten years. Since then, he has established himself as the most prestigious scholar researching the affects of Agent Orange/dioxin on humans and the environment.

In his words: "As a physician of the military forces of Viet Nam, when I lived with the troops in the jungles, dozens of times American planes attacked us spraying dioxin over a vast area. We knew it was dangerous, but the Agent Orange mist enveloped the whole Truong Song mountain range. We had no place to hide; we could only stand and wait for the blow of death.

"After the war, I hovered between life and death, tortured by illness caused by Agent Orange. My wife and children were also affected by terrible illnesses. My wife gave birth three times, but all the children were deformed, and finally they died."

For himself, it was as if he had died too. But he was alive. He chose to live for each person, to find the truth for those still suffering.

For the next thirty years after the end of the war, Dr. Le Cao Dai devoted himself to researching the damaging effects of Agent Orange and dioxin. He met thousands of veterans and youth volunteers who had been exposed to Agent Orange during the war. He visited many areas throughout the South and Central Highlands and other heavily sprayed areas for research. A healthy man would find this hard work. But Dr. Le Cao Dai himself was always ill, carrying his illness with the weight of the world on his back. For three months, he worked in the A Sau and A Luoi districts of Thua Thien Hue Province in the Central Highland. He surveyed the defoliated land and took samples from the soil, water, and human beings to be analyzed later in a lab. The results of these tests quantified the damaging effects of the dioxin in Viet Nam and stunned scientists from around the world. The doctor explained: "My work forced the American researchers to enter the game. By this time, prestigious scientific institutions around the world, such as the American Academy of Sciences and the World Health Organization, had recognized eleven diseases—cancer, cerebral palsy, deformities, and others—as common results of exposure to dioxin. We made a map of the areas most heavily sprayed with Agent Orange and marked the fifteen with the highest concentrations of dioxin: the A Sau, A Luoi, and A So districts of Thua Thien Hue Province, the Bien Hoa airbase, etc. A test of the soil around Bien Hoa determined the dioxin concentration to be one thousand times higher than the minimum safe level stipulated by the World Health Organization."

We followed Dr. Le Cao Dai for a month-long trip visiting victims of Agent Orange and dioxin in the A Sau and A Luoi districts and several other southeastern provinces of Viet Nam, places where he had already conducted some research.

At Bien Hung lake—whose water before contamination had been a deep blue—a dirty, gray viscous scum stretched from shore to shore. The lake is about one kilometer from the Bien Hoa airbase in Dong Nai Province, where, during the war, the American military had stored Agent Orange. Every day, American planes left this base on their missions to spray the toxic herbicides throughout the south of Viet Nam. After the war, the Americans went home to their country, leaving the storehouse of poisonous chemicals still there. A unit of Vietnamese troops built a wall around the contaminated storehouse to keep people from getting into this dangerous area. The wall could stop human beings from getting in, but not the weather. With each heavy rain, dioxin flooded from the storehouses and airbase to the lake and surrounding areas, contaminating everything it touched, including the fish. Then the fish and the water poisoned the people.

Dr. Le Cao Dai showed us some test results and explained: "The concentration of dioxin in the soil of Bien Hoa airport is one thousand times higher than the maximum safe level established by the American Environmental Protection Agency. Many people who lived in the area around the airport and the lake have already died. We've just finished testing 159 human samples, of which 142 showed very high dioxin concentrations in the blood, with levels ranging from 275 to 285 PPT. That's 135 to 140 times higher than normal."

Mr. Vu Huu Dang and his family live very close to the lake. When we arrived at his house, he and his wife and son were sitting under the shade of a mango tree. Dr. Le Cao Dai had come here many times, so he was well acquainted with them. Pleased to welcome the doctor and a reporter to their home, Dang's wife, Mrs. Hoa brought tea and tobacco to us in the cool beneath the mango.

Before us sat a family of three: Mr. Dang, Mrs. Hoa, and their son, who was about twenty years old. Mr. Dang's sallow face swelled with edemata; red blistery sores covered his arms and legs; and in other places his skin appeared to be sloughing off. Mrs. Hoa's pale face wore a look of confusion; her eyes were sunken. The son looked emaciated, tired, and very sad. Three people, three parts of the many affected by dioxin.

Dr. Le Cao Dai gestured toward them and said:

"Mr. Dang's family here is in the group of families with the highest levels of dioxin in their bodies. Mrs. Hoa has a level of 271 PPT, 130 times higher than that of normal person, and Mr. Dang has a level of 168 PPT, 80 times higher than normal. Their son was born more than ten years after the end of the war, and now, at twenty years old, he has a dioxin level of 95 PPT, 40 times higher than normal. This situation is indeed precarious. It has afflicted them with serious illnesses, and it has made the family have to struggle simply to survive."

Before visiting Mrs. Hoang Thi Thuy's family at Village 3, Phuoc Hiep Commune in Phuoc Long Province, Dr. Le Cao Dai told us that when he had first come to see Mrs. Thuy three years ago, he had brought a Dutch scholar with him. Both he and the Dutch scholar had been horrified when Mrs. Thuy's daughter appeared. Her name was Nguyen Thi Hoan, and she was about thirty years old. A big flap of meat covered the left side of her face. A deep hole penetrated the lower part of her forehead. When viewed in profile, it seemed she had three eyes. Below the flabby meat, a semi-circular hole looked like a toothless mouth. The flab caused so much suffering: it always ulcerated, bled, and hurt her terribly.

Mrs. Thuy said: "At the time peace started, in July 1975, I was carrying my eldest child. Listening to people talk, we all thought the people living in the area around the American's chemical weapons might be contaminated or might give birth to deformed kids. I was really afraid. One day, I went to see the fortune-teller in Phuoc Long and asked him if my future had anything strange in it. After praying and making obeisance to the spirits of his house, the fortune-teller stared intently at my belly. He did not speak or laugh, and when his two eyes seemed stuck to the place they looked at, I began to feel strange, worried for myself. Calmly, I asked, 'What problem must I face?'

"The fortune-teller still didn't say anything. After another minute or two, he jerked up his chin and said, 'There is a very strange baby in your belly!'

"Hearing that I had a child in my belly filled me with terror, and I trembled uncontrollably. I asked under my breath:

"'Strange how?'

"The fortune-teller didn't answer at first, his eyes still locked on my belly. Then he said, 'Your baby's face is ferocious as a demon's.'

"I couldn't believe it. I shouted, 'Oh God! Can that be true? What can I do?'

"The fortuneteller told me to make ceremonial offerings immediately. 'It might change the situation,' he said. 'With heaven's help, you might give birth to a good child, but without it, the devil you'll give birth to will be very bad.'"

"After that, I was haunted always by the fortune-teller's terrible prediction. When calm returned, I could occasionally convince myself it wasn't true, that it couldn't be true since my husband and I were kind-hearted people and a good turn deserves another. A devil-face baby could never get into my belly. Time went by and eventually I became pregnant. With the fortune-teller's warning on my mind, even while writhing on the bed in agony, I kept staring between my legs, desperate to see my child's face. When it appeared, I screamed and fainted."

And now, thirty years later, here was that child, a grown woman. Though Dr. Le Cao Dai had described Nguyen Thi Hoan to me in detail, when we met I still couldn't believe my eyes. I could never have imagined such a strange face. If all her life all she had to do was carry this huge face, Hoan could do it, but the flap in and of itself was just the start of the problem. She also had an ulcerated wound that bled and gave her interminable pain all the time.

Mrs. Thuy said: "It's been thirty years she's had a face like this, always with this fluid and pus running out of it like you see today. I apply medicine every day, but still the blood leaks. She lives her life from day to day, but it's been very hard for us, Uncles!

"During the war, my family lived in Binh Phuoc Province. In those days, the American planes often came to drop bombs and sometimes sprayed poisonous chemicals near the villages. After the spraying, many people became seriously ill and died. My husband and I lived, imagining ourselves to be lucky. But whoever breathed those toxic chemicals has kept them in their bodies a long time. Our family also died with those people back in the village because we have a daughter just as unlucky as they were."

After visiting Mrs. Thuy's family, we accompanied Dr. Le Cao Dai to visit Mr. Le Thanh Can, who lived at the Phuoc Thiep Communal House in the Cu Chi District of Ho Chi Minh City. During the war, Mr. Can was wounded by shrapnel, as well as contaminated by Agent Orange, which blinded him in both eyes and caused the death of three of his children.

When we arrived, Mr. Can came from his lemon orchard into the yard. With one hand resting on his wife's shoulder, he groped with the other to find his way. His wife helped him to sit on a bamboo bench on the porch, and each of the visitors brought out a stool from inside the house. With all of us sitting around, Dr. Le Cao Dai asked about Mr. Can's health and about the health of his son.

"He just lays in bed," said Can, "completely oblivious."

I asked him, "How were you exposed to Agent Orange?"

Can turned his face toward us, his blind eyes winking as if he could see us, and said: "On that day, planes launched attack after attack at our jungle outpost. Then our commander told us planes were coming to spray poisonous chemicals. Following protocol for a toxic attack, we covered ourselves with pieces of nylon and lay on the ground. After the planes passed, we got up, took off the nylon, and discovered that some of it had been eroded by chemicals and was full of tiny holes. The chemicals had filtered through to our heads and necks. Others had gotten chemicals in their eyes, and it hurt them terribly. My own eyes swelled up; then they gradually became dim, and after a while, I couldn't see anything at all."

After resting a moment, Can continued: "The American poison was so wicked. Six times the American planes sprayed our unit lying there. A lot of us, especially the younger ones, got sick and died. My children kept hoping I'd get my sight back, but I knew all along my future would always be dark."

Can fell silent for a long while, trying to suppress the pain and misery in his heart. When he regained his composure, he said: "After the war, I was demobilized, came back to my home town, and got married. My wife had four children, but all of them had deformities and disabilities. The bodies of the first three were covered with ulcers and hair. They are all dead now. My youngest son, Kiem, lying over there, is the only survivor. He is paralyzed and mentally ill as well. Though paralyzed, he doesn't lie there quietly; instead he tosses constantly, sometimes crying, sometimes laughing. I'm blind but I have to try to look after him. Looking after a child who's mentally ill, a child who's paralyzed, who's incontinent . . . it's very hard."

"According to Dr. Le Cao Dai's test results," I said, "we know the concentration of dioxin in your body is 125 times higher than normal, and you are seriously ill. Do you have any request for the government?"

"We have been recognized by the government as Agent Orange victims," said Can, "so we receive a pension, but it is very little money for medical treatment. I know our government is very poor and can't offer us more than that. But I want to ask the Americans for compensation for the Agent Orange victims. They have to be responsible for what they've done in the war." Can's voice grew more indignant.

"I have sent many letters to the American government and urged the producers of the deadly chemicals to come to Viet Nam to see and know how my family and many other families have suffered endless pain and distress. They could not ignore the hard facts with so many victims as living witnesses of their crime."

For over a month, Dr. Le Cao Dai led us on visits to forty-two families suffering from Agent Orange exposure in Dong Nai and Binh Duong Provinces and in Ho Chi Minh City. These families have played a large part in Dr. Le Cao Dai's Agent Orange and dioxin research. Forty-two families, forty-two fates, but each will suffer a death from dioxin. None of them have had a different experience with their children from that of Mrs. Thuy's family in Phuoc Long or Mr. Can's family in Cu Chi.

After returning to Hanoi, we were invited by the Viet Nam Red Cross to meet James Zumwalt, who is the son of Admiral Elmo Zumwalt Jr. Admiral Zumwalt had given the order to spray herbicides along waterways in South Viet Nam. He had not expected the terrible consequences of his decision. When the Americans sprayed the toxic chemicals on the vast forests and rivers of South Viet Nam, one of his sons, James's older brother Lieutenant Elmo Zumwalt III, was on patrol in one of the sprayed areas.

As the saying goes, *He who lives cruelly, dies cruelly*. The dioxin in Agent Orange not only poisoned the Vietnamese people, but also many American veterans, including Lt. Elmo Zumwalt III and his son, Russell.

In their joint memoir, *My Father, My Son*, which has been translated into Vietnamese and published by the National Politics Publishing House in Hanoi, Admiral Zumwalt describes the tragic situation of his family: "Because of the orders I gave to step up defoliation in the

Ca Mau Peninsula around Sea Float, there is no question in my mind that, indirectly at least, I was responsible for Elmo's heavy exposure to Agent Orange, which makes me an instrument in his tragedy . . . What has happened to Russell and Elmo deepens my own sense of futility about the Vietnam War, and makes its memory all the more painful for me. I regard Elmo and Russell as casualties of that war."

Lieutenant Zumwalt was indeed one of the war's victims. In *My Father, My Son*, he wrote: "I believe Agent Orange is responsible for my cancers, for Russell's learning disorder, and for illnesses suffered by many Vietnam veterans. . . . Soon after the onset of my second cancer, Dad and I visited the Pentagon and examined a map showing the areas of heaviest spraying in Vietnam. About 5 to 15 percent of the country was sprayed with Agent Orange, and I had spent much of my time in two of them, Da Nang and Sea Float. But in virtually every combat area I patrolled in Vietnam, there was evidence of defoliation."

The truth is like this. Tens of thousands of people have died from these poisonous chemicals, and millions of people live on the edge of death. But the American government and the chemical companies that produced these deadly herbicides have ignored their responsibility for the effect of these products on the victims in Viet Nam. Admiral Zumwalt seems to be the only person aware of his responsibility. Too old and too weak to travel abroad, he sent his youngest son to Viet Nam to do charitable work and to help him make amends for his decision.

In a talk with Dr. Le Cao Dai, James Zumwalt, the director of an Agent Orange victims foundation,*said: "My friends and I are work-

*While James Zumwalt did make this trip, he is not and was not the director of an Agent Orange victims foundation. He is, however, a special advisor to the Thurman-Zumwalt Foundation, which "supports biomedical research into infectious and toxic agents," especially those whose use affects U.S. military personnel.

ing hard to raise public concern in America about the Vietnamese people who have been affected by the Agent Orange used by the American military during the Viet Nam War. My father's health is too poor to make his wish for visiting Viet Nam come true. My father and his friends have expressed deep regret at the pain and distress of our family and of the families of many Viet Nam veterans. He said that the most fatal mistake in his life was to command the spraying of toxic herbicides in South Viet Nam. This decision also led to the death of one of his sons and severe learning disabilities in a grandson. The purpose of my trip to Viet Nam this time is to fulfill the hopes of my father for visiting and expressing great regret to the Agent Orange victims in Viet Nam. We continue to work hard to establish some support for them."

After the long trip visiting Agent Orange victims in the South, we received the bad news that Dr. Le Cao Dai had been rushed to the army hospital. The dioxin in his system had made him a very sick man. At the hospital, a physician told us that the concentration of dioxin in Dr. Le Cao Dai's body was 215 PPT, 100 times higher than normal. After several days, he could no longer resist the specter of dioxin and quietly passed away.

For over thirty years, Dr. Le Cao Dai established good relationships with the victims of Agent Orange, something not just anyone could do. He was a scientist, but he was also the director of the Agent Orange Victims Fund. He wrote dozens of valuable articles about his dioxin research and a book titled *The Consequences of Agent Orange in Viet Nam*. The book resulted from his hard work of many years, during which he traveled to many contaminated areas and visited many exposed people all over the country. His studies and evidence have attracted the attention of many scientists and lay people from all over the world, announcing clearly: America sprayed dioxin-laced Agent Orange in Viet Nam; Americans cannot refuse to take responsibility for causing such pain and destruction.

As a physician, from the very beginning, Le Cao Dai had a strong desire to help the victims of Agent Orange. He gave them good and wholehearted medical treatment. For thirty long years, he worked hard to help the war's victims, but in the end the one victim he could not help was himself.

Hanoi, 2005

TRANSLATED BY HUY LIEN AND CHARLES WAUGH

CONTRIBUTORS

HOANG MINH TUONG:"GRACE" AND "THE STORY OF A FAMILY"

Hoang Minh Tuong was born in 1948 in Dong Phi village, Ung Hoa District, Ha Dong Province. He graduated from the Faculty of Geography, Hanoi University, and began work as a teacher and journalist. At present, he is the vice director of the Creative Writing Department of the Vietnamese Writer's Union.

His several novels include the Writer's Union Prize winners *Someone Walking along the Different Road* and *Water, Fire and Gangsters*, as well as *The Hard Wind which Follows the Storm*, *An Illegitimate Child*, *A Beautiful Lady*, and the controversial novel on the 1960s land reform, *The Days of Saints and Gods*.

MA VAN KHANG: "A CHILD, A MAN" AND "THAY PHUNG"

Ma Van Khang, one of the most eminent and famous writers of Vietnam, was born in 1936 in Hanoi. As a teenager, he joined the People's Army of Vietnam to fight in the resistance war against the French. He is a graduate in literature from Hanoi Pedagogical University and was the headmaster of a high school in Lao Cai Province. In 1975, he became editor-in-chief of the Labor Publishing House and *Foreign Literature Review*. His publications include many novels: *The Summer Rain*, *The Season of Fallen Leaves in the Garden*, *The Wedding without Marriage Certificate*, *The Orphans in a Selfish Community*, *Against the Flood*, and *A Lonely Person Driving a Lonely Horse*. He has published some two hundred short stories, of which many have been anthologized and translated into Russian, English, German, Japanese, and Swedish. In 1998 he was a winner of the ASEAN's Literary Prize.

MINH CHUYEN: "A FATHER AND HIS CHILDREN" AND "LE CAO DAI AND THE AGENT ORANGE SUFFERERS"

Minh Chuyen was born in 1948 in Minh Khai Commune, Vu Thu District, Thai Binh Province. During the Vietnam War, he joined the army and fought along the Cambodian border for more than ten years. Now he works as a scriptwriter and documentary film director for the VTV network. As a veteran who fought in the American War for many years, most of his nonfiction essays are on the war and, in particular, on the life and suffering of the many veterans and their families affected by Agent Orange. His literary works include short story collections such as *The Native Land of the Soldier* and *The Woman He Met in his Dream* and many nonfiction collections such as *A Wanderer Who Doesn't Feel Lonely*, *The Aftereffects of the War*, *The Consternation*, *Vietnam in the Postwar Period*, and *The Soul and the Heart of Agent Orange's Sufferers*.

Minh Chuyen was a winner of many prizes for literature and television documentaries, including several prizes from international television festivals.

NGUYEN QUANG LAP: "THE GOAT HORN BELL"

Nguyen Quang Lap was born in 1956 in Quang Binh and has published many plays, literary essays, and books, including *The Call of Sunset*, *Black and White Lives*, and *The Life of Sand*. At present, he is an editor at the Kim Dong Publishing House.

NGUYEN THI NGOC HA: "THE SPIRIT POND"

Nguyen Thi Ngoc Ha was born in 1949 in Ba Dinh District, Hanoi. After graduating from the Hanoi Commercial College, she joined the faculty there and at the same time was an employee of the Hanoi import-export company Intimex. In 1990, she retired from the college and the company and now concentrates on writing poetry, short stories, and nonfiction. Her publications include several collections of poetry published by the Writer's Union Publishing House and Hanoi Literature and Art Publishing House. Many of her short stories and essays were published by the prestigious *Literature and Art* magazine. She has won several literary prizes awarded by the *Literature and Art Weekly*.

PHAN NGOC TIEN: "A DREAM"

Phan Ngoc Tien was born in Hanoi in 1956. He joined the People's Army in 1972 and fought along the Cambodian border before joining the Ho Chi Minh campaign from 1974 to 1975. Now he is a scriptwriter and film editor at the VTV network. His works include a collection of short stories on the American War, *They Become Real Men*, that won the Writer's Union prize in 1994, as well as *Black Ashes and Red Dots*, *Waiting for the Sun*, *The Little Creature*, and *Native Village*.

SUONG NGUYET MINH: "THIRTEEN HARBORS"

Suong Nguyet Minh was born in 1958 in Yen My village, Yen Mo District, Ninh Binh Province. He joined the army in 1977 and was a member of the forces who fought along the Cambodian border before battling into the interior and overthrowing the Khmer Rouge. Since then, he has attained the rank of colonel and now works as an editor of *People's Army Literature and Arts* magazine. He is a graduate of the Land Forces Officers' training school and the Faculty of Literature, Hanoi University. He has published several short story collections, including *Trong Nhan Village at Night*, *Villagers of the Chau River Harbor*, *Thirteen Harbors*, *Passing through the Fields in the Afternoon*, and *Love Market*. The Youth Publishing House, the Education Publishing House, and the Ministry of Defense have each awarded his collections first prize.

THU TRAN: "THE QUIET POPLAR"

Thu Tran was born in 1963 in Bien Hoa City. At present she is the editor of *Contemporary* magazine in Ho Chi Minh City. She is a member of the Writer's and Artist's Union of Ho Chi Minh City and a member of the Writer's Union of Vietnam. Her publications include the short story collections *The Old-Fashioned Master, Four Persons Whose Bodies Are as Light as Leaves,* and *The Return of a Changeable Wind* and the novels *A Sacred Lake, It Seems that We Are no Longer Teens,* and *A Lady and Her Beautiful Hair Appear on the Sidewalk.*

TRUNG TRUNG DINH: "LOVE FOREST"

Trung Trung Dinh was born in 1949 in Vinh Long Commune, Vinh Bao District of Hai Phong City. At seventeen he joined the army and fought from 1968 to 1977 before enrolling in the Nguyen Du school for creative writing. He worked as editor of *People's Army Literature and Arts* magazine from 1983 to 2003, the vice editor-in-chief of the Writer's Union's *Literature and Arts Weekly* from 2003 to 2006, and vice director of the Writer's Union Publishing House from 2006 to 2008, which he now directs. He has published many short story collections, including *Nights at Dak Hoa Valley, People Trapped in a Dirty Plot, A Night of Lunar Eclipse, A Highly Capable Opponent,* and *The Separation of the Stars.* His novels include *The People Who Never Surrendered, A Dark Alley, People Lost in Thick Woods, To Live Is More Difficult than to Die, Making Last Farewells to Unhappy Days,* and *The Other Side of Death.* In 2007 he was awarded Vietnam's literary National Prize.

VO THI HAO: "THE BLOOD OF LEAVES"

Vo Thi Hao was born in 1956 in Dien Chau District, Nghe An Province. A graduate of the Faculty of Literature, Hanoi University, she has worked as an editor of the Ethnic Culture Publishing House. She is also a journalist and a talented painter. But her greatest achievement is in the field of fiction writing. Her publications include many short story collections and novels, such as *Salvation Sea*, *Black Widow*, *The Last of the Comedians*, *The Stories that Should Not Be Read at Midnight*, and *The Pyre*. In 2006, Vo Thi Hao became the first Vietnamese writer to establish and run her own culture and media company.

TRANSLATORS

HUY LIEN is the pen name of Nguyen Lien. He is emeritus Professor of American Literature and Vietnamese Culture at the Faculty of Literature, College of Social Sciences and Humanities, Vietnam National University. He is a literary critic, editor, and translator in addition to being a scholar. His research interests include American culture and American literature. He has translated many works of American literature into Vietnamese and is the author of dozens of essays of literary criticism. In 2000, he was a coordinator and organizer of the first International Conference on American Literature in Vietnam.

LENA LE was born in 1984 in Thanh Tri village in Hanoi, Vietnam. In 2007, she graduated from the Department of International Studies at the College of Social Sciences and Humanities, Vietnam National University, then joined the faculty as an English language lecturer. In addition to her work on this volume, she also works as a freelance translator for the *Vietnamese Student Magazine*. Currently she is pursuing a master's degree in international affairs at Australian National University.

TRAN THI QUYNH HOA was born in Hanoi in 1984. She completed her undergraduate work at the Department of International Studies at the College of Social Sciences and Humanities, Vietnam National University in 2006 and then joined the faculty as a lecturer of English. In 2007, she earned a Ford Foundation fellowship to pursue a master's degree in international relations and Southeast Asia studies at the School of Advanced International Studies (SAIS),

Johns Hopkins University. Following her graduation from SAIS in May 2009, she returned to the faculty at VNU.

CHARLES WAUGH grew up in a small town in Ohio and first lived in Vietnam in 1996. His stories and essays have appeared in *Flyway*, the *Sycamore Review*, the *Wisconsin Review*, *Knock*, *Proteus*, *Studies in American Fiction*, and *ISLE*. He teaches fiction writing and American studies courses at Utah State University and is the fiction editor of *Isotope: A Journal of Literary Science and Nature Writing*. In 2004 he received a Fulbright Fellowship to join the faculty at the Vietnam National University in Hanoi, where he helped develop undergraduate and graduate programs in American studies, taught a course in the literary, cultural, and environmental history of the U.S., and delivered the first lectures on ecocriticism in Vietnam.

CREDITS

Hoang Minh Tuong's "Grace" was originally published as "Duyên" in *Literature and Arts Weekly*, Ocober 8, 1996. "The Story of a Family" was originally published as "Chuyện một gia đình" in *Army's Literature and Arts Magazine*, August 1992. Both are reprinted by permission of the author.

Ma Van Khang's "A Child, A Man" was first published as "Heo may gió lộng" in *High Wind* (*Heo may gió lộng*) (Hanoi: Writers Union Publishing House, 1984). "Thay Phung" was originally published as "Thày Phùng" in *The Writers' Magazine*, September 2002. Both are reprinted by permission of the author.

Minh Chuyen's "A Father and His Children" was originally published as "Cha và con" in *Literature and Arts Weekly*," December 4, 2005. "Le Cao Dai and the Agent Orange Sufferers" was originally published as "Di chứng chất độc da cam" in *People's Army*, July 27, 2005. Both are reprinted by permission of the author.

Nguyen Quang Lap's "The Goat Horn Bell" was originally published as "Tiếng lục lạc" in *Perfume River* (*Song Huong*), April 1985. It is reprinted by permission of the author.

Nguyen Thi Ngoc Ha's "The Spirit Pond" was originally published as "Đầm ma vầy" in *Literature and Arts Weekly*, September 1, 2009. It is reprinted by permission of the author.

Phan Ngoc Tien's "A Dream" was originally published as "Giấc mơ" in *People's Army*, March 20, 1974. It is reprinted by permission of the author.

Suong Nguyet Minh's "Thirteen Harbors" was first published as "Mười ba bến nước" in *Literature and Arts Weekly*, September 25, 2004. It also was published in a collection of his short stories titled *Thirteen Harbors* (Hanoi: Youth Publishing House, 2006). It is reprinted by permission of the author.

Thu Tran's "The Quiet Poplar" was originally published as "Cây phong non âm thẩm" in *The Labourer*, July 7, 2006. It is reprinted by permission of the author.

Trung Trung Dinh's "Love Forest" was originally published as "Cánh rừng tình yêu" in *Young People*, June 21, 2005. It is reprinted by permission of the author.

Vo Thi Hao's "The Blood of Leaves" was originally published as "Máu Của Lá" in *Literature and Arts Weekly*, June 25, 2005. It also was published in *A Survivor from the Laughing Forest* (Hanoi: Women's Publishing House, 2005). It is reprinted by permission of the author.

LaVergne, TN USA
13 August 2010
193131LV00002B/1/P